Unclaimed Heart

Daniel S. Christensen

Minneapolis, MN

Join Our Community

$\vdots$

For updates on new material, please:

'Like' on Facebook:
www.facebook.com/StudioRemarkable

or

Subscribe to the RSS feed:
www.studioremarkable.com

or

Follow on Twitter:
www.twitter.com/studioremark

Copyright © 2012 by Daniel S. Christensen
Cover photos copyright © 2012 by Daniel S. Christensen

First Edition, 2012

Published in the United States of America.

Unclaimed Heart

1:
Fall

1

Seth first noticed her over lunch at the Park College cafeteria.

The cafeteria's serving area was crowded with students who were gathering their food between classes. A dense scattering of tables and chairs occupied a space immediately beyond the main serving area. Most of the available chairs were filled by students, their conversations blending together into a symphony of jumbled voices.

Seth sat with three friends - Mark, Dave, and Tony - at a round table, situated directly off of the food serving area. The day had been like any other for Seth, with classes all morning. His hour long break at noon allowed him the opportunity to catch up with his closest friends.

Mark was Seth's roommate and the person most responsible for connecting the group. Mark had known Seth and Dave since freshman year, when they had all been lab partners in a tough introductory Biology course. They would not have ordinarily picked one another as friends, but they bonded over petri dishes and microscopes and had remained close ever since.

Mark was a jock and had met Tony through the college baseball team. Over time, Mark had managed to 'grandfather' Tony into the group of friends. As time went on, Tony became the 'mouth' of the group.

Like Mark, Tony was also athletic and a lady's man. Unlike Mark, Tony was rough around the edges. Seth was not as close to Tony as he was to Mark or Dave, but they still hung out together. Seth admired Tony's confidence, even if his crassness sometimes made Seth cringe.

Dave was the friend who Seth always thought would go on to become a millionaire. He was the 'analytical one' in the group. While Seth was considered an exceptional student, particularly in classes related to his Biology major, Dave was a whiz in mathematics classes.

Rather than conversing about their day's events, Seth and his friends were making observations about the other students passing by their table.

"Bagels guys," Tony said, clearly excited by a female student who had caught his eye. "She's over at the BAGELS!"

"Where?" Mark asked. "Which one Tony?"

Mark looked around with no success. While Seth considered Mark to be a good person, he always seemed to be one step behind during most conversations.

"The hot one you idiot," Tony said. "Tina."

Tony's tone communicated disbelief that Mark could not identify a beautiful girl standing right in front of him. Mark continued searching for the girl, still not spotting her.

"Mark," Tony continued, offering help. "How can you not see legs like that when she's leaning against the counter?"

When Mark finally located 'Tina,' he scoffed. Seth wasn't surprised since Mark had complained in the past about Tony's habit of exaggeration.

"She's too plain," Mark said, turning back to his food. "There's nothing going on there."

"What does that mean?" Tony asked. He sounded shocked. "Too plain! A woman has to be a supermodel to register on your radar."

Tony looked over at Dave, who was taking notes on his tablet computer. Dave turned his attention back to the scenery, seemingly oblivious to the argument between Tony and Mark.

"Her stock's shooting up?" Tony asked. "Right Dave?"

Dave responded without breaking his stare from the crowd.

"It's up." Dave confirmed. "But it's still not recovered from that dip she took last weekend."

"What dip?" Tony asked, clearly worried that he had not been privy to a recent piece of crucial information.

"The one it took when I saw her crawl out of my roommate's bed Saturday morning," Dave said. "Any girl getting into a bed with that hairy beast takes a hit."

Tony and Mark looked wide-eyed at one another. Mark, reeling from Dave's bombshell, tried to get Seth's reaction.

"Hey Seth," Mark said.

Seth was still settling into his lunch. He resisted joining what had become a routine amongst his friends.

In fact, Seth had skipped the past several lunches with the guys for just that reason. He was too busy to waste time on idle gossip. Of course, his absences had not gone unnoticed.

"And where have you been?" Tony asked Seth. "Too good to eat with your boys anymore?"

"I needed to get a jump on my med school applications," Seth said, paying more attention to his food than the conversation.

Dave also tried to engage Seth.

"You need to look up from a book sometimes to see the beautiful world passing you by," Dave offered.

"Especially the beautiful people," Tony said. "Over there, Jessie Johnson by the toaster. Where's she trading at today?"

Tony motioned to Dave's tablet computer, but Dave did not bother looking away from the girl.

"Trading up already," Dave said. "If Miss Johnson keeps that skirt on for the rest of the day, she might reach an all-time high."

Seth tried to stay above the fray. "You guys still on that stock market crap?"

"Damn right," Tony said. "The market's been like a bull all week. Spring skin is in the air. We're even thinking of expanding things."

Dave glanced over at Seth, who only paid him partial attention. He then gave his sales pitch to Mark.

"It could be huge if we got more guys involved," Dave said. "We're thinking we could all make a little money on the side. What guy wouldn't want to play a market based on young ladies?"

Before Mark could respond, Seth offered his own analysis.

"You don't foresee running into any problems?" Seth asked.

"What do you mean?" Dave countered, obviously confused.

"When the women find out," Seth said. "The ones whose

reputations you're trading on with your little venture aren't going to be very amused."

Tony, being the 'sales guy' of the concept, was unmoved. He suggested a way to work the situation to their advantage.

"If the money's good enough," Tony said. "Maybe we can pay off some of them. Bring them on board."

Seth shook his head. "You're a visionary Tony."

"Thanks." Tony said, oblivious to Seth's sarcasm. "I'm not just thinking of myself here."

Seth continued with his sarcasm. "Oh?"

"It's about every guy who has ever needed some guidance..." Tony said.

Tony's voice trailed off as Seth became distracted by shifting students in the crowded serving area. A sea of people parted and, for an instant, a beautiful girl locked eyes with Seth.

Seth was stunned by the sight of the girl. He interrupted Tony in midsentence.

"Who is that?" Seth asked, dazed.

Dave looked around. "Who? Who is who?"

"That girl over there by the juice machine," Seth said.

Tony sat back, smiling.

"You're on this campus for three years," Tony said. "And you don't know who April Jordan is?"

"I've never noticed her," Seth admitted.

Park College had an enrollment of four thousand students, making it not as anonymous as a large university. However, at that size it was still not a place where everyone knew one another. Complicating matters, Seth was constantly studying instead of socializing. He hated to admit it, but the constant distractions meant that he rarely met new people.

"Dave," Tony said. "Tell the man about Miss Jordan."

"Miss April Jordan," Dave said, looking at his notes. "Senior, single. We think alone for quite a while. An enigma. Never any news or dirt. Solid blue chip rating."

April glanced at the seats available in the commissary. She quickly settled in at a small table with one other girl.

"Why no boyfriend?" Seth asked, still watching April.

"Not sure," Dave said. "Her stock is stable, mostly because we don't get much information on her."

"I've seen her around," Mark said, offering his first words

on the topic. "Seems like a nice girl."

Seth was taken aback that his own roommate would know about April, yet he had never mentioned her. Granted, Mark had a girlfriend, but that didn't mean not commenting on attractive women around campus. If anything, he usually never missed an opportunity to needle Seth into pursuing such a prospect.

"She's one of those unapproachable women though," Mark said. "She doesn't go out much. When she does, she's with her own posse."

Seth assumed that Mark was referring, at least in part, to the girl whom April was seated with. Seth didn't recognize that girl either, but the more that he studied her, he realized why.

While April's appearance was the definition of a 'classic' beauty, her friend could best be described as a 'hippie.' Students like April's friend associated with people in different circles than Seth. They tended to live off-campus together.

Unlike many colleges or universities, the majority of Park College's students lived on campus through their senior year. Much of that tendency had to do with convenience, but was also due to a general lack of off-campus housing. The town of Winneshiek, where Park College was located, only had a limited number of rental units nearby the college campus.

"They keep every guy away," Tony said with a hint of frustration in his voice.

Tony stood up to leave, but he paused to smile at Seth.

"Nice to see you paying attention," Tony said. "Next time, look for someone who you've got a shot at."

"What's that supposed to mean?" Seth asked, annoyed by Tony's dismissal.

"You aren't the first man to have an eye for Miss Jordan," Tony said. "And you won't be the last."

2

Seth and Mark finished eating and left the cafeteria together. They followed a flow of other students up a bank of stairs. The campus cafeteria had a terrific view of the nearby valley, but it was essentially in the basement of the student union.

The stairs from the cafeteria led to the union's main level, where students zigged and zagged along a long, central hallway. Some headed into a campus coffee shop, while others walked into the bookstore. Still others were on their way to the college's administrative offices.

It was at one such intersection that Seth noticed April again. She merged into a pack students headed toward the union's central exit.

When Mark also spotted April, he was quick to point her out to Seth.

"Beautiful timing," Mark said, nudging Seth.

Seth's eyes followed April through the crowd with relative ease. As Seth walked a few yards behind April, he noticed something drop out of the side of her jacket pocket.

"She dropped something," Seth said. He was not sure what had fallen, but he became determined to rescue it for her.

No one else in the hallway had noted the fallen article. Seth quickened his pace to its location.

When Seth reached the item, Mark stood nearby and watched Seth retrieve it. Seth inspected the object for a moment, obviously thoughtful.

It was a set of keys.

"What're you planning on doing with those?" Mark asked. His voice contained a mix of curiosity and worry.

Seth knew that if either Tony or Dave were in his position, they might do something stupid with the keys. Instead, Seth had a straightforward strategy.

"I plan on returning them to the lady," he said.

Mark's face lit up. "Maybe get a little reward from Miss Jordan?"

Seth shook his head at Mark, feigning annoyance over the implication. He could not hold back his happiness over the lucky break for long though, eventually giving Mark a sheepish grin.

After leaving the student union building, Seth continued to follow April. He'd nearly lost track of her while retrieving the keys and lagged far behind. He walked fast, but could not catch up with her until she was literally outside of her dorm room door.

As Seth burst around a far-off corner that led him toward April's dorm room, he watched her arrive at her doorway. She reached into her pants pocket for her keys. When she didn't find them, she appeared flustered.

"April!" Seth said, yelling from far down the hallway. "Are you looking for these?"

Seth held April's keys in hand. He hustled down the narrow corridor.

April seemed surprised by Seth's sudden presence and eagerness. She didn't appear afraid of Seth though. If anything, her first reaction looked to be one of relief.

"My keys!" April said happily. As Seth handed them to her, a hint of awkwardness emerged. "Where did you find them?"

Seth thought fast, trying to come up with an answer that didn't make him sound like a stalker.

"You dropped them in the union," he said. "I finally caught up with you".

April took the keys from Seth and used them to unlock her door. They worked as expected and April began to enter her room, but then stopped. She turned back to Seth and smiled.

"Have we met somewhere?" April asked. "You knew my name."

Seth panicked for an instant before regaining his composure.

"Um..." Seth stalled. He knew that his answer could make

or break his chances with April. "We had a class together a couple of years ago. I think Biology."

"I've never taken a Biology class," April said.

Seth's response came out quickly, his body almost-subconsciously trying to extract himself from the nervous encounter. "It might have been something else. Anyway, I'd better get going."

April didn't seem overly eager to let him leave.

"Then I'm sorry to ask," she said. "What was your name?"

"Seth," Seth said. "Seth Peterson."

April looked as though she was trying hard to recall the name, but it did not register.

"I'm sorry," she said.

"It's not a big deal," Seth assured her. "People always say that I blend into a crowd."

Seth continued to worry about appearing nervous. He knew enough about women to assume that April was accustomed to guys constantly flirting with her. To his surprise though, she didn't seem put off by him, at least not yet.

"Thank you very much Seth Peterson," April said. "You saved my day."

Seth's mind raced for something memorable to say in closing.

April added. "I hope that we run into each other again."

Seth was blown away by what seemed to be an invitation, but he was not smooth enough to capitalize on it. In his mind, he was already celebrating what he thought to be a substantial victory in interpersonal relations.

"Yeah," Seth said as he left. "I'm sure that we will."

3

Later that afternoon, Seth returned to his dorm room to study. He stretched out on his sofa and settled in for what he expected to be a long night of work. At least, he had intended to study hard. That was going to be a difficult task, with his concentration distracted by thoughts about his unlikely encounter with April.

Not long after he had become comfortable on the sofa, Seth's wandering train of thought was interrupted by a frantic knock at the door. The sudden noise caused him to jump.

"Come in," Seth said, collecting himself.

The door burst open. Tony strutted into Seth's room, giddy with excitement. He dribbled a basketball as best one could on a carpeted floor.

"Did you score?" Tony asked, ignoring normal pleasantries. "Did you buddy? You have to tell me."

Based on the first few seconds that Tony had been in his room, Seth knew that the visit would only waste his time. He tried to brush Tony off, not acknowledging the question.

"You can trust Tony," Tony continued, unable to suppress what had become his trademark grin.

Seth knew that he could most certainly not trust Tony to keep gossip under wraps.

In contrast, Seth had thought that he could trust Mark. He was surprised that Tony already knew about his encounter with April and was disappointed with Mark for evidently leaking the day's earlier events.

Seth played dumb. "What're you talking about?" He hoped that Tony might leave.

"April," Tony said. "April Jordan."

"What about her?"

"Mark told me that you found some of her keys and brought them by her place. I figured maybe you worked some of those old Peterson moves on her."

Seth finally looked up from his book, giving Tony an annoyed look.

"You haven't been up to our room in over a month," Seth said. "And this is why you're interrupting me?"

Tony threw his basketball at Seth, who caught it at the last instant. Seth continued staring with his irritated gaze.

"Hey," Tony said. "I'm just trying to help."

"You're not helping," Seth said.

"I'm just curious," Tony said, not knowing when to quit. "That's all."

Seth exhaled with a deep sigh.

"All I did was drop off the keys," he said.

Tony smiled, hoping that Seth might finally be opening up.

"And then she invited you in..." Tony started.

"And then nothing," Seth said. "She thanked me and I left."

"You always pull this man," Tony said. "First you knock a woman dead. Then the girl nearly forces herself on you and you chicken out."

"That's not what happened at all."

Tony kept pressing Seth. "What're you afraid of?"

Seth didn't like being called a coward and his irritation with Tony grew.

"I'm not afraid." Seth said. "You don't understand the situation."

Seth chucked the basketball back at Tony.

"No," Tony said. "I think I do understand the situation."

Seth stared at Tony without replying. Tony continued, relating his own spin.

"You're afraid you'll get locked into something," he said. "But it doesn't have to be like that."

"So you're suggesting that I make it my goal to use her," Seth said. "Then I should dump her?"

"I've made a lot of very nice women happy that way Seth,"

Tony said. "Commitment is all in the mind buddy. What's wrong with playing the field a little? How do you expect to date anyone if you don't ever ask them out?"

Seth shook his head. Crass or not, he knew that Tony had a point. Just the same, that logic didn't stop Seth from feeling defensive. Even if he was being irrational, he was not going to budge.

"Just because I'm not following women around like a lonely dog doesn't mean that I'm not interested or not looking," Seth said.

"What is it then?" Tony pressed. "You're letting the prime of your life slide by."

"I just don't want to waste my time with girls who I know I don't have a future with."

"This isn't about the future," Tony said. "It's about what you need to take advantage of right now."

Seth sighed. "What if I knew right away that I'd end up breaking it off with her or what if she breaks it off with me? Where would I be?"

"You'd be safely out of the situation," Tony countered. "Besides, how do you know with such certainty anything about a girl you won't even take the time to ask on a date?"

Seth reflected on the circumstances for a moment. His thoughts drifted back to his freshman year at Park College.

"I just don't want a repeat of what happened with Sheila," Seth said.

"That was three years ago," Tony said, dismissively. Seth knew that he had no tolerance for references to Sheila. None of Seth's friends did. "She was a psycho. It was the best decision of your life when you dumped her."

Seth looked over at a collage of photos and picked the tiny image of Sheila out from amongst the numerous other faces of friends, past and present. He'd never entirely let her go and his current friends had long-since gotten tired of hearing about her.

Seth had met Sheila during the summer prior to first leaving for college. They'd worked together at the same summer job and had both noticed a natural chemistry. Sheila was a year older than Seth and struck him as much more 'experienced.' Her having spent a year at a local university had intimidated Seth, but he never admitted that to anyone.

It was only a few weeks after starting college that Seth noticed Sheila drifting away from him. Seth told his friends that he had broken up with her, but that wasn't the case. He'd gotten dumped. It still stung three years later. He found himself replaying the pivotal events in that brief relationship and second-guessing his every action.

Seth knew that his continued fixation was pathetic, but it was a convenient crutch. It was also much more comfortable to retreat into his studies than risk failing with other girls.

"There are still days when I regret doing that," Seth lied, keeping intact the longstanding explanation of his breakup with Sheila. "I invested a lot in her."

"And she didn't invest jack into you," Tony said. "You were doing all of the work."

"Maybe," Seth said. "But I could have done something more."

"Stop overthinking that man," Tony said, getting irritated. "I can't believe that you've even got me talking about this again."

Seth skipped the basketball back to Tony. He had grown weary of the conversation and wanted to wrap things up.

"My whole life is riding on the choices that I make in the next few weeks," Seth said. "If I lose focus, I can kiss med school goodbye."

"So you'll have plenty of time to meet new people when you're cutting them open?" Tony pointed out. "You're never going to have an opportunity again to meet women like you do right now in college."

"I'm not even in April's league," Seth said, returning to their original subject. "Every guy on this campus would kill for her."

"Oh," Tony said. "So you're afraid."

Seth shook his head.

"Whatever," he muttered. "I don't think that you understand."

Seth started shutting down. Tony walked over to the dorm room's door and opened it wide, but then stopped.

"Look man," Tony said, softening his tone. "Maybe this is for the best."

"What's that supposed to mean?" Seth asked, suddenly feeling confused. He wasn't sure about Tony's intent. As had been the case at lunch, it was unclear to Seth if Tony was challenging him or encouraging him to drop his interest in April.

"Like I said to you earlier," Tony replied. "April's been around and hurt her share of guys. I don't want to see you get hurt Seth. I don't. You're right that you haven't dated much, so she's maybe not the best girl to get back into the game with."

Tony stepped out of the room, slamming the door shut behind him.

4

Park College's football field was a far cry from that of many colleges' football stadiums. A low collection of bleachers sat along one side of the field, meant for the visiting team's fans. On the opposite side, a much large bleacher construct rose up with several dozen rows of benches for the home fans.

The home fans did enjoy a majestic view of the campus's surrounding river valley from their vantage point. That was usually the best part of the football viewing experience.

Football was not a star attraction at Park College, but the team had done unexpectedly well in their season that autumn. As such, fans packed the home stands for the latest gridiron showdown. The cloudy Saturday afternoon had produced fluffy snowflakes, but not enough to accumulate on the faded grass field.

Seth, Tony, and Dave were part of the home crowd. They sat together in the last row of the home bleachers, high above the field.

"There is no way that we can let those hicks from Central win again." Dave said.

Central was usually the favorite in Park College's athletic conference. They had won the conference championship on a nearly-annual basis.

Seth glanced at the scoreboard. The Park College Jayhawks were up 14-13 over Central and time was running out. Unfortunately for the Jayhawks, Central's players were setting up for a field goal.

"If I were still playing," Tony said. "We wouldn't be in this situation."

Seth scoffed at the remark. Tony always brought up such claims when they were at tight games.

"Why was it again that you got cut?" Seth asked.

"I didn't get cut." Tony said. "I quit because I wasn't getting the respect that I deserved. It wasn't worth my time."

Seth was never entirely sure about the truth behind Tony's claim. He had tried repeatedly to get the facts out of Tony regarding his unexpected departure from the football team during the prior season. Even Mark didn't entirely know the full story. Sometimes finding the truth with Tony was like going down a black hole.

Seth glanced down at the crowd below and noticed a face looking up at him. It was April. He smiled and waved, unsure if she was gazing at him or someone else in the crowd.

Seth couldn't read anything from April's reaction and grew self-conscious. He stopped waving, flashing back to a mishap during his freshman orientation. He had waved across a room at a newfound friend, only to have the wave intercepted by a random, annoyed girl. Such actions could be dangerous.

"This is ridiculous," Dave said, indicating the probable loss of the game due to the play that was about to unfold.

As the players moved into position, the crowd rose to their feet. Seth lost his view of April when she became blocked behind a wall of bodies. Dave continued yelling, his voice somehow managing to rise above many others in the crowd.

"Mark!" Dave yelled. "Knock it down!"

Moments later, the ball was snapped. A particularly fast Park College defender broke through the offensive line and leapt into the air. He managed to catch the football an instant after it was kicked.

The defender tucked the ball under his arm and sprinted across the open field. Several of Central's players raced after him. They could not close the distance to him in time. The Park College player strode into the end zone, scoring a touchdown.

"Credited with the touchdown is number eight," an announcer said. "Linebacker Mark Bernard."

The Park College players and coaches all ran onto the field in celebration. Members of the crowd raced into the end zone to join them. The home team's fans were ecstatic.

"Yes!" Dave screamed. "I love you Mark!"

Amid the celebration, the crowd thinned. Seth looked back to where April had been standing. She was no longer there or anywhere in the vicinity. She had disappeared.

5

By the following Monday, Seth's studies had, as usual, taken priority. It was set to be a busy week for him, starting with an exam that afternoon. After a brief lunch, he headed to the library to review his notes.

Seth had spent most of the prior weekend studying for the exam, trying his best not to think about April Jordan. As the weekend had passed, a sense of urgency slowly helped him focus. With the exam scheduled during his first afternoon class, that urgency hit its peak.

As Seth made his way out of the student union, he weaved through a mob of fellow students. He didn't pay attention to any of the faces in the crowd, so he was startled when he heard a female voice say, "Hi Seth."

Seth looked around in surprised confusion until he noticed April. She waved over and gave him with an inviting smile. Seth cut his path to her, moving with a bit of uncertainty.

"Hi," Seth said. As had previously been the case, he was immediately nervous and still startled by the randomness of the encounter. Taken off guard, he had no idea what to say. "Small world, huh?"

"Yeah," April said.

"Do you usually go this way?" Seth asked. "I've never noticed you walking along here before."

"Not after lunch," April said. "I'm meeting a friend here now. Have you eaten yet?"

Seth's heart raced. If there were any time in his life that he would have wanted to lie and eat two consecutive lunches, it would have been that moment. Unfortunately, Seth knew that his impending test would need to take priority.

"Actually," Seth began, trying to come up with a compromise. "I have a test in my chem class, but maybe…"

Seth was cut off by the appearance of several long foam pillars that haphazardly crossed in front of him. He'd been so distracted in his conversation with April that he had not noticed several students carrying the pillars in his direction. Despite nearly being knocked over by the team of students, Seth was quick to recover as they passed.

"What the heck was that?" Seth asked.

"They must be setting up for the ball." April said. "Are you planning on attending?"

Seth remained distracted and only half-thinking in his reply.

"I'm not sure," Seth said. "I was thinking of getting some med-school stuff out of the way."

April looked disappointed, so Seth backpedaled. He knew that he was quickly destroying any chance that he might have with April. He had not meant to sound evasive, but his life was so structured that anyone not knowing otherwise would assume that he was avoiding them.

"I'll try to stop by," Seth said, abruptly correcting course. "I should be able to get everything done by then."

April's expression lit up.

"It'll be a lot of fun," she said.

April looked over her shoulder as a female student approached. She was the same 'hippie'-type girl whom Seth had noticed April eating with in the past.

"Kassie," April said, providing introductions. "This is Seth."

Seth nodded and smiled, as did Kassie.

"Are you joining us?" Kassie asked.

"I wish that I could," Seth said, reiterating his earlier explanation. "But I need to get ready for a test."

Seth felt uncomfortable with the look that Kassie gave him. In his mind, Seth was sure that he was being evaluated, perhaps for later discussion with April. True or not, that was what he imagined and it caused him anxiety.

"I'll see you at the ball then?" April asked again.

"I'll try," Seth said.

After leaving the student union, Seth changed course down the sidewalk. The clock continued to tick until his exam. Glancing at his watch, he realized that he no longer had time to study in his usual spot at the library. Instead, he walked rapidly in the direction of the sprawling science building, hoping to find a quiet corner there.

As Seth neared the science building's entrance, Dave ran to catch up with him. Dave startled Seth when his hand grabbed onto Seth's shoulder.

"I almost yelled over to you a minute ago," Dave said. "Then I saw you standing with Miss April Jordan. What was all that about?"

"Nothing," Seth said. "We bumped into each other on the way over. I was being polite."

Dave didn't seem to buy the explanation. Like all of his friends, Seth knew that Dave was hoping for more salacious details to emerge.

"Oh come on," Dave said. "I was starting to believe what you fed Tony about nothing happening with April at her room. Then I saw that."

Seth knew that he was losing precious minutes that he could be using to study for his exam. He didn't have the time to waste sparring with Dave.

"Why is it that every time a guy is talking to a girl," Seth said. "He wants to sleep with her?"

Instead of apologizing, Dave doubled-down.

"Calm down man," he said. "Speaking from my experience, that's usually the case."

"I need to get going," Seth said, again looking at his watch.

By this point, Seth and Dave had arrived outside of the science building's main entrance. Seth pulled open one of the entrance doors.

"The only time it isn't true is when the girl is ugly," Dave said. "Miss Jordan isn't ugly."

Seth gave Dave a cold look.

"I don't have time to talk," Seth said as he entered the science building. He looked back over his shoulder and saw Dave still standing outside, giving him a smile and two thumbs up.

6

While the evening after the chemistry exam might have meant a time to relax for many, Seth did not take a break. His test had seemed to go fine, but it quickly became an afterthought. Seth had been holed up since dinner in his favorite study spot, a wooden booth-style desk at the end of a row of similar desks. It was located in a far corner of the college's library basement.

Seth's spot in the library was well-known by his friends, even if they only visited it infrequently. That particular evening, he had been left alone. A pile of books related to his medical school entrance exam were spread out in front of him.

The peace that Seth had enjoyed was interrupted when Tony emerged from behind a row of book shelving and sat down at a desk next to Seth.

Seth ignored him, focusing on a particular book.

"Don't play this game," Tony said. His tone was like a pouting puppy dog. "Talk to me buddy."

After failing to get Seth's attention, Tony reached over and closed Seth's book.

Seth looked up angrily and asked. "Don't you ever study?"

"Uh-oh," Tony said, switching back to his normal self. "Somebody's getting cranky. You don't even know what I want to talk about."

"It'll be the same thing you guys have been talking about for the past two days." Seth said.

"Hey," Tony said. "We're only trying to help you out."

"And how exactly have you been doing that?" Seth asked. "By badgering me about April? By pressuring me to chase after someone on a whim?"

Tony waved his hands.

"Just a second," Tony said. "You think that we're using you for our own amusement?"

"Yes," Seth said. "I do. This is your entertainment."

Tony paused to think for a moment.

"Maybe a little," Tony said. "But that isn't the main reason. We want you to be happy. We're here to help you."

Seth wasn't buying Tony's remarks. He knew that Tony was only visiting on a 'reconnaissance mission,' hoping to pick up nuggets of gossip.

"I don't need your help," Seth said.

"You do," Tony said. "But you haven't realized it yet."

Seth re-opened his book, trying to send a message to Tony that he wanted to get back to work.

Tony didn't seem to get the hint though. He continued. "You always act like you have life all figured out."

"Maybe I do," Seth said. "It's called planning for the future and it's what successful people do."

"That's you limiting your options," Tony said. "I'm not planning things out and look how happy I am."

Seth scoffed. "We'll see how happy you are in about nine months when you move back in with your parents and get a job at a convenience store."

Seth had previously tried to have conversations with Tony about his future, but his advice never seemed to stick. On a good day, Tony seemed genuinely eager to get his act together. In time though, such efforts had always quickly faded.

For reasons never clear to Seth, Tony could not help but live in the moment. Reinforcing Tony's behavior, he was smart enough to get away with that approach. In fact, he slid through his management classes with relative ease.

Unlike most of Seth's friend's, Tony had a backup plan. That was what seemed to sap much of his motivation. His father owned a small manufacturing firm and Tony could easily take a sales position there after graduation. Seth hated to admit it, but that job might end up being a decent fit for Tony.

"You do have a bug up you today." Tony said. "Don't you?"

"Yeah," Seth said. "It's named Tony."

Tony sat back in his chair and laughed at the retort.

"It's just that I heard that you were taking April to the ball this weekend," he said. "Any truth to that?"

Seth wasn't sure how Tony knew anything about April mentioning the ball. The knowledge somehow didn't entirely surprise Seth though.

"I'm not taking her," Seth said. "I don't even know if I'm going."

"Interesting," Tony said. "That's not what I'd heard. And that surprised me, you know?"

"No," Seth said. "I don't know."

"It's just that we'd talked about it and I figured that you'd realized that she wasn't your kind of a girl."

Seth didn't take the bait, but Tony pressed. "That's what you thought, right?"

"We're friends Tony," Seth said. "Sometimes I don't know why, but you and I are friends. Even though that's the case, I don't think that you're the best guy to be taking dating advice from."

Tony seemed mock offended by the dismissal.

"So what do you plan on doing?" Tony asked.

Seth continued to want the conversation to end and thought that he might finally have that opportunity.

"It's not that I don't want to get to know her," Seth admitted. "It's just a terrible time for it to happen."

7

The next morning, Seth attended the first session of a special course that would run throughout the latter half of his fall semester. As Seth walked into the appointed classroom, he passed by his advisor Professor Tashiro Lee. Lee handed Seth a stack of notes.

"Can you do me a favor Seth?" Lee asked, pointing to a diagram in the notes. "I need that transposed on the board."

Seth nodded, honored in knowing that Lee didn't trust most other students to assist him.

Lee was the head of the Park College biology department. He was a slight man, shorter than many of his students, with sharp features. Seth frequently observed that Lee always wore a white lab coat, sometimes forgetting that he had it on and walking around campus with it.

While Seth worked at the board, he noticed Jim Jenson, the college's associate dean of curriculum, approaching the room. Seth knew that Lee had been friends with Jenson for years, so he was not surprised by the visit.

Jensen went straight to Lee, presumably for a brief conversation. Several other students squeezed behind Jenson to get into the room, the period set to start in another minute. Given his proximity, Seth could overhear the conversation that ensued between the two men.

"Are you sure that you want to take this on?" Jenson asked. "I know that you've already taken a full class load. We could still have someone else on the staff split it."

Lee looked around. There were students in only fifteen of the room's thirty desks.

"It's fine Jim," Lee said. "I enjoy teaching this class more than any other."

Out of the corner of his eye, Seth noticed Jenson motioning at him. Jenson spoke in hushed tones to Lee, but they were standing at such an angle that their voices continued to carry in Seth's direction. Seth felt uncomfortable eavesdropping on their conversation, but there wasn't much that he could do about it.

"Is he the one?" Jenson asked.

Lee seemed confused. "Who?"

"The kid at the board," Jenson said.

"Seth?"

"Yeah" Jenson said. "I wasn't sure if I recognized him. He's your genius?"

Seth tried unsuccessfully to prevent his face from turning red in embarrassment. He kept drawing on the board, hoping that none of his classmates were also overhearing the conversation.

"He probably has the most potential of any pre-med student to come through here in ten years," Lee said.

Jenson seemed impressed by the high praise. "Really?"

"He's easily surpassed everyone else in the class," Lee said.

Jenson gave Lee a half-hearted ribbing. "You aren't worried he'll burn out are you? You do have to keep those med school entrance numbers up."

Seth knew that Professor Lee was frequently under pressure from the college's administrators to ensure that he maintained impressive professional school placement numbers. So far as Seth had observed though, Lee did not focus on that objective. Instead, he seemed to sincerely desire that his students succeed for their own sake.

"Seth won't burn out," Professor Lee said. "He's accomplished every goal that he's set for himself under my advising. He won't fail to reach the biggest one of all."

Jenson left the room as Professor Lee walked over to Seth. Lee took back his notes and motioned for Seth to take a seat.

Professor Lee finished writing his name and contact information in large letters on a board at the front of the room.

Having completed his final preparations, he began his lecture.

"I recognize all of your faces," Lee said. "But if you've forgotten, and I hope that you haven't, my name is Tashiro Lee. This won't be a normal class, but instead these sessions will prepare you for the medical school entrance exam."

Professor Lee turned from the board and stepped up to a podium.

"You all realize that medical school admissions are very competitive," Professor Lee said. "Does anyone know how many medical schools there are in this country? Barry?"

Barry, seated behind Seth, was eager to answer.

"Two Hundred?" Barry said.

"No," Professor Lee said. "There are only 125 medical schools in the United States."

From his podium, Professor Lee moved to get his actual content for the class arranged. In the meantime, he carried on with his introductory banter.

"46,000 people applied to those 125 schools last year" Professor Lee continued. "Only 15,000 were accepted. Look to your left and look to your right." "Only one out of three of you will get in."

Professor Lee knew from experience that that statement would capture the students' attention. He turned on a projector. Several statistical tables appeared on the screen behind him.

"If we look even deeper into the statistics," Professor Lee said. "Only 6 percent of those who get into medical school will actually get into your first choice school."

Satisfied that he had made his point regarding the challenges still ahead for the students, Professor Lee turned off the projector. He then went back to the board, where he wrote a list of course names.

"These were your core classes," Professor Lee said, indicating an initial grouping of courses. "All of you should have already taken them or had best be taking them sometime this year."

Professor Lee next drew a long line down the middle of the board. He made a note at the beginning.

"This is where we are now," he said. "Next week is the first of November and we have the final seven weeks of this semester."

Lee moved further down the line and drew in another

spot.

"This is when you'll take the MCAT," Professor Lee said. "The Medical College Admission Test. As you all know, you need to take that exam in order to apply for medical school."

Professor Lee scribbled in the area between the first and second points that he had drawn.

"You should plan to take the test by early February," Professor Lee said. "Between now and winter break, we will use this class for review. However, I hope that you listened to my advice last year and were disciplined enough to begin preparing during this past summer."

Lee wrote a third mark onto the board, making it appear like a bull's-eye. It was placed shortly after the MCAT's exam date.

"Your applications will be due at most medical schools no later than March," Professor Lee said. "Get started on those applications now."

Professor Lee pulled a large book from his bag and held it up. It was an MCAT study guide. Seth, along with several of his peers, already had it open on their desks. A few other students reached into their bags to retrieve it.

"If you don't have any questions," Professor Lee said. "I'd like to begin the review."

The class sat in silence. Seth looked around and noticed that most of his classmates appeared concerned. Seth felt uneasy after the wave of information, but he was determined and ready to take on the challenge.

8

After his MCAT prep class, Seth went back to his dorm room. He had expected to meet his friends for dinner. As he entered the room, he discovered Mark hard at work studying his football video game.

Mark's attitude toward his schooling was more like that of Tony than Seth. While Seth was often uptight about his schoolwork, Mark was riding through college on mediocre grades. Unlike Seth though, Mark had a relatively balanced life, with his time shared more evenly between his studies, social, and athletic pursuits.

Melissa Morris sat next to Mark, reading from a textbook. Melissa was Mark's girlfriend and had been so for over two years. Seth had heard stories about Mark dating a string of girls during his freshman year in college, but the pair had been together for as long as Seth had been roommates with Mark.

"The ladies' man is home," Mark said.

Although Seth found Mark clever at times, he often felt that Mark used that cleverness in misguided ways. Mark came across to most as a good-looking and not brainy jock, but he was actually quite adept at cheerfully winning people's favor. Seth thought that in a future life, Mark's ability to slide between personas might make him a decent politician.

"Jeez," Seth said. "Not from you too."

"Hi Seth," Melissa said. "Sorry about stupid's big mouth."

Melissa hit Mark with a pillow. He blocked her blow while still playing the videogame.

"Calm down woman," Mark said. "You'll mess up my game. Sorry man, word travels fast."

"I've noticed," Seth said, still annoyed that Mark had participated in gossiping about April amongst his friends.

Seth and Melissa had always gotten along well. She often helped to keep Mark in check, providing a mature voice in times of need. She had also tried, at various intervals, to set Seth up on dates. When Seth did not react well to those overtures, Melissa gave him his space. Still, if given the opportunity, she could not resist encouraging his romantic pursuits.

Melissa could also be flirty, but Seth assumed that that attribute was part of her charm to Mark. She kept him on his toes.

"Melissa," Seth said. "Are you working on any new ways of motivating him to study?"

"No," Melissa said. "I gave up on that a long time ago."

Mark scoffed at the notion.

"I don't need to study," he said. "I study and learn what I need to know. It's not that hard."

This was a new defense by Mark.

"Huh?" Seth asked.

'You don't need to read all those books that they tell us to buy," Mark said.

Seth laughed at the comment while unloading his backpack.

"Oh," Seth said. "So you're learning by osmosis now?"

"If you take notes you'll get what you need," Mark said. "Usually there are some old tests to refer to and then you can rally some smart people into a study group. Do all that and you're set."

"You don't sometimes think that maybe you're missing the point of college?" Seth asked.

"Actually, I think that I have it all figured out. College is more than just books and classes my friend. There are more important things in life."

"Like me," Melissa said.

"Right," Mark said. "Like this beautiful creature."

Melissa again threw a pillow at Mark, this time managing to knock away his video game controller.

"Flattery doesn't mean that I let you play videogames all day stallion," Melissa said. "Let's go before they close."

"The things I do for love Seth," Mark said, getting up to turn off his video game console.

Seth watched as both Mark and Melissa put on their

jackets.

"Where are you guys going?" Seth asked. He'd gotten distracted by their conversation and momentarily forgot why he had come back to his room in the first place. "What about dinner?"

"We have to go down to Aumannson's to pick up my tux," Mark said. "You know, for the ball."

"You want us to pick yours up too?" Melissa asked.

Seth didn't immediately answer. He knew that he would be in trouble.

"You're going to the ball," Melissa continued. "Right?"

"Actually," Seth said. "I didn't rent one yet. I wasn't sure if I would need it."

"That's what Tony was saying," Mark said. "You're making a big mistake Seth."

Seth gave Mark the same excuse that he'd just given to Tony. "It's just a bad time for me to think about dating someone."

Seth braced for Mark's reply, anticipating that he would have one. Unlike Tony, Seth knew that Mark was wholly encouraging of Seth pursuing April.

"That's when these kinds of things always happen," Mark said. "At the absolute worst times. How much of college have you missed out on because you were constantly studying?

"That's what I have to do," Seth said. "I've worked too hard to see everything fall apart because I got distracted at the end."

"Don't think of this as a distraction," Mark said, switching gears. "It's an opportunity. A chance for you to see what you've been missing."

"I know what I've been missing," Seth said.

"No," Mark said. "You don't. And when you get a taste, maybe you'll realize how miserable you've been without her."

"You'd better just come down there with us," Melissa said. "If you're lucky, they'll still have something to rent."

The small town of Winneshiek was located immediately adjacent to the Park College campus. The college's staff and students accounted for a large percentage of the town's ten thousand person population. It was an older community, having been established by settlers from various western European and Scandinavian countries. Winneshiek's river valley location lent it forests of trees and steep hills.

Winneshiek's most prominent constructed feature was a classic main street. The shops that lined that street had throwback flair to them. Many attracted tourists on the weekends.

Aumannson's Clothing was located in the middle of that cluster of stores. The nearest clothing stores were nearly an hour drive from Winneshiek, so Aumannson's was known for servicing the local community. The owners also helped students at the college by keeping prices at modest levels on certain items.

Inside the store, a salesman stood behind Seth's shoulder as they both stared into a mirror.

"Sorry," the salesman said. "This is our last one. If you'd come in sooner, we might have had some other options."

Seth was decked out in a bright white tuxedo that was far from flattering. Nearby, Mark watched the salesman try to tighten up the tux with pins. It had been too late for Seth to get it altered, so the temporary solution would have to do. Melissa stood at Mark's side looking dismayed over the situation.

"You know what they say," the salesman said. "It's not the clothes that make the man."

"The man can make the clothes buddy," Mark added, giving Seth a thumbs up. "And this man will be making a lot for himself."

Melissa evaluated Seth's tux from a distance. As the salesman pinned certain parts to fit into place, its appearance marginally improved.

"It doesn't look that bad," Melissa said, clearly hoping to boost Seth's confidence. "Just a little unusual. Some girls like that."

"Get a last-minute date?" the salesman asked, making conversation while he worked.

"No," Seth said. "I just decided that I wanted to go."

Melissa walked over to browse the shoe selection. Mark peered at her and waited until she was out of hearing range before putting his hand on Seth's shoulder.

"Now Seth," Mark said. "Don't lie to the man."

Seth looked on with suspicion, wondering why Mark needed to discuss his situation while they were waiting.

"Tomorrow night," Mark said. "My roommate here steps down a golden road for the first time in... how long has it been?"

Seth winced. "Would you shut up and help me out?"

Mark whispered over to the salesman. "Let's just say that it's been a little while."

"Everything's set," the salesman said, stepping aside. "Except for your shoes."

The salesman went over to a shoe rack near where Melissa was browsing. He rummaged through a storage box, pulling out a flashy pair of shoes that he then presented to Seth.

"I'd been saving these for a buddy" the salesman said. "But since he hasn't shown up to claim them, I'll give them to you instead."

"Thanks," Seth said, trying to convince himself that he had somehow caught a break. "Maybe they'll draw attention away from the tux."

The salesman took the paper packaging from the shoes and helped Seth check if they fit.

"It's always a dog and pony show that we have to put up with for women," the salesman said.

"Tell me about it," Mark said. This time, he didn't speak softly. Melissa shook her head in reply.

The salesman took the jacket off of Seth. Seth headed into a dressing room to change out of the remainder of the tuxedo.

"I've been seeing a girl off and on," the salesman said. "She's a senior at Park, so I've had to go through all this myself."

"You'll be at the ball tomorrow?" Seth asked from behind the dressing room door.

"Yeah," the salesman said. "I have to go to make her happy. I wouldn't put up with half of the stuff she pulls if she wasn't so crazy in bed."

Seth peered over the dressing room door at a wide-eyed Mark. Melissa looked angry at the comment but held her tongue.

Seth emerged from the dressing room in his normal clothes and handed the outstanding pieces of the tuxedo to the salesman. The salesman bagged it all up.

"Thanks for the rental," Seth said as he completed the transaction at the check-out counter. "Maybe I'll see you tomorrow."

"Good luck with that girl," the salesman said.

9

The night sky was clearly visible from inside of Park College's activity center lobby. Seth admired the sight through the wall of glass windows that formed the lobby's main entrance. It distracted him one last time before walking further into the building.

The fall 'Harvest Ball' had been an annual tradition at the college for decades. This year, it was being held in what amounted to the campus gymnasium. During basketball season, the gymnasium was used as a tiny arena, but for the ball it had been decorated reminiscent of a prom.

Seth moved into line with other people who were waiting to enter the main dance area. He caught flashes of activity inside the darkened room through a small set of lobby doors.

From across the sea of heads around him, Seth spotted Tony waving at him. Seth gave Tony a half-hearted smile and braced for Tony's reaction as he approached.

"That tux doesn't look half as bad as Mark said it did," Tony said.

Seth shook his head. Even when Tony tried to be helpful, it often came out sounding wrong.

"That isn't helping me," Seth said.

A quick glance around the area confirmed that Seth was wearing the only non-black tux in sight.

"It'll make you stick out more though," Tony said. "You know, call attention to yourself."

Seth grimaced. "That's the opposite of what I had in mind."

"Hey now," Tony said, trying to cheer up his friend. "You

look good."

The line into the main dancing area suddenly moved ahead much more rapidly and Seth spotted his other friends dancing inside.

"I see Dave and Mark," Seth said to Tony, wanting to get on with the evening and not dwell on his shortcomings.

As Seth and Tony took their first steps into the gymnasium, they wove through the crowd of people to meet up with the rest of their group.

The event was wildly popular, with people packed close to one another. Throngs of people were dancing to the beat of the music. The music was loud inside the main dancing area. Everyone had to yell in order to communicate.

Seth and Tony slid past bodies to make their way over to a small circle of people near the center of the dance floor. That was where they finally caught up with Mark, Melissa, and Dave. Their group was filled out by several other students whom Seth also knew casually.

When Dave noticed Seth, he stepped back to the outside and hugged him.

"Seth my man," Dave said. "You are looking good tonight. But you've got to get loose."

Seth could smell a faint whiff of alcohol on Dave's breath. Dave was usually an affectionate person, but it was clear to Seth that he was extremely gregarious that evening. Not surprisingly, Dave soon reached inside his tux and pulled out a small flask. He took a quick swig from it and then passed it over to Seth.

"Taking it straight's the only way to go," Dave said.

Seth hesitated, but out of courtesy took a quick swig.

"You can do better than that," Dave said.

Seth did not drink. At least not much or very often. Even if he had the time to party, which he did not, he had never gotten into that scene.

Most of Seth's friends began drinking during their junior and senior years in high school. Seth's parents had not been drinkers though and seemed to disapprove. After many of Seth's high school friends had a large party busted by the local police, drinking had not seemed like much fun.

When Seth arrived at college, drinking amongst the students was certainly not unusual. It was not a focal point of the campus culture, but, like most institutions of higher learning, it was an activity that occurred at Park College.

Occasionally, Seth played along to avoid hassles from his friends. It was sometimes easier than arguing with them, at least to a point.

"No," Seth said. "You don't want me to drink your share."

Dave was too drunk to argue. His attention span was limited, so his priority quickly changed back to the topic of dancing. "Let's see those old Peterson moves."

Before Seth could respond, Dave gave Seth a shove into the middle of the dance circle. Since Seth had never learned how to dance, being the center of attention was something that he had wanted to avoid.

Seth made a few awkward attempts at dance moves, still annoyed with Dave for pushing him into the spotlight. Seth's circle of friends cheered him on as he tried to make the best of it. The entire exercise lasted less than thirty seconds before Dave decided that he wanted the spotlight for himself.

"Get over here," Dave said, pulling Seth out of the circle and taking his place. "Let me show you how it's done."

Dave moved into the middle of the circle, where it was obvious that he loved to dance for the crowd. Dave twisted out a series of relatively easy moves to the pounding music. After going through the routine, he motioned to Seth, encouraging him to imitate what he had been doing.

Seth realized that Dave was trying to help him out and went along with the lesson. The dancing circle of friends collapsed into a smaller cluster. With less of a spotlight on him, Seth felt more comfortable working on improving his skills.

Dave and Seth spent a few minutes going over basic moves. Seth grew more comfortable as he loosened up. He was, not surprisingly, a fast learner and soon had a couple of moves down. It was not much, but it gave Seth more confidence in an otherwise uncomfortable situation.

As the next song hits its climax, Seth glanced over his shoulder and froze at what he saw. April was standing across the dance floor. Seth had gotten so distracted with his friends that he had momentarily forgotten to search for her at the ball.

As Seth stared over at April, her eyes meet his. She cut across the crowd toward him. Seth lost his relaxed demeanor. His mind raced to anticipate how the encounter might play out.

One thing that Seth knew: He did not want April around his friends. Not yet. To avoid making things even more awkward for him, Seth moved away from the guys and toward April. A few second later, Seth and April met one another amid several large clusters of students.

Because of the loud music that continued to play, Seth and April shouted to one another as they conversed.

"You look nice, "April said. "I thought that maybe you were more into the traditional, but it's nice."

Seth couldn't tell if she was being truthful or polite about his tuxedo. If it was the former, April was proving to be quirkier than he had assumed. In his experience, girls like her tended to seek conformity, but she seemed to be defying that trend.

"I wanted to be different," Seth said, playing along.

"That," April said. "I could already tell."

Seth paused for a moment, not knowing what to say. He'd seemingly been successful in getting past his main source of anxiety for the evening – his appearance – and April was still standing with him.

"Your dress looks fantastic," Seth said.

There could be no debate over that topic. April's dress did indeed look fantastic. It was an unpretentious, yet stunning dress. In Seth's mind, April looked like the most beautiful girl he had ever met.

"Thanks," April said. "It's been hanging in my closet forever. I never get a chance to wear it."

Seth looked around and realized that he and April were the only two people not dancing.

"Do you dance?" Seth asked.

"No," April said, throwing Seth for a loop. "Can you show me some pointers?"

Seth remembered that he had just learned a thing or two that he could share. With an ease that surprised himself, Seth repeated the moves that Dave had shown him. April copied the moves, but the pair did not have long to dance before the song came to an end.

After a brief silence, a slow tune began. Couples around

them paired up. Seth knew that he had to make his move.

"Do you want to..." Seth asked, not entirely getting the words out.

"Sure," April said.

April reached out to Seth. After Seth had fumbled his hands into position, the pair began to dance together.

Seth couldn't remember the last time that he had slow-danced with a girl. He thought that it must have been sometime in high school. In college, thankfully he thought, dances had been rare. Park College held a formal ball in the late fall and another late in the spring, but he had never previously attended either.

At first, Seth struggled to get his bearing. He looked around and noticed Mark and Melissa smiling over at him. He also spotted Dave dancing with an unknown girl, flashing him a thumbs up.

Turning his full attention back to April, Seth realized how much he enjoyed holding her. She was shorter than him, small in build, but she felt right in his arms. Seth looked into her eyes while she leaned next to his ear.

"I shouldn't tell you this," April said. "But my friends warned me not to hang out with you."

Seth was immediately curious about the admission.

"Why?" he asked.

"It wasn't anything to do with you," April said. "I think that it had something to do with a friend of yours."

Seth had an idea who she might be talking about, but he asked the question anyway. "And just who would that be?"

"A guy named Tony Engel," April said. "He picked up a friend of mine at a bar one night and never called her back."

"That sounds like Tony."

Seth was relieved that April seemed to already understand that he was different from his friends. At the same time, he was frustrated that his friends' behavior might be a bigger liability than he had realized.

"He's hit on me a couple of times too," April said. "But I've always brushed him off."

"I wish more girls did the same," Seth said.

"Don't worry about it." She winked at Seth. "I like being around a dangerous guy once in a while."

Seth didn't immediately understand the joke. He had

always heard that beautiful women seemed to go for the 'bad boy' types. As such, his sense of inferiority made his mind momentarily race. April threw her head back in laughter at his worried reaction and the pair continued dancing. Seth smiled, his confidence in the situation having been firmly built up.

Seth's guard began to fall as he realized that he had misjudged April. She continued to defy his expectations. He could still hear a quiet voice in the back of his mind, urging him not to become distracted with a relationship. As much as Seth was enjoying being with April though, such internal debates were easy to ignore for the time being.

As the evening played out, Seth eventually found himself seated with April amid a row of chairs next to the dance floor. They had gone from dancing to having an engaging conversation that made Seth lose track of the time.

Seth almost fell out of his chair as he reacted to a story that April was in the middle of telling.

"...and then what did you say?" Seth asked.

"I just looked at her and said 'Put that cantaloupe down right now!'" April said.

Seth continued laughing. "That is the funniest thing I've ever heard!"

"Yeah," April said. "Can you believe it?"

April paused, turning her head. Seth noticed that she appeared distracted. He looked in the same direction as her, but couldn't tell what or who had caught her attention.

"Hey," April said. "Can you wait here? I just saw someone come in."

"No problem," Seth said. He was confused by the interruption, but he'd had such an enjoyable time with April that he didn't think much of it.

April stood up and pushed her way through the crowd. At the same time, Mark walked over and sat in the newly-empty chair next to Seth.

"Chase her off already?" Mark asked.

"No," Seth said. "She'll be back in a minute.

Seth looked around.

"Maybe you'll have disappeared by then," Seth continued.

Mark gave Seth a disappointed look.

"Hey now," Mark said. "I was wondering where you'd snuck off to without me. What's been happening over here?"

"We've been talking," Seth said.

"You need the room tonight?" Mark asked.

Seth looked annoyed at Mark.

"I don't think so," Seth said.

As the crowd shifted, Seth and Mark's view across the dance floor opened up. Seth spotted a glimpse of April. He could tell that she was talking to someone, but that person was standing out of sight.

Seth continued to feel confident and softened up enough to admit to Mark what a wonderful evening he had been having.

"She's a lot different than I'd realized," he said.

While Seth spoke, he kept his attention in April's direction. Bodies shifted around April as a taller man was revealed to be standing next to her.

"Hey isn't that the jerk from the rental place?" Mark asked.

Indeed it was. April was talking to the salesman who had helped Seth pick out his tuxedo earlier in the week.

April looked up at the salesman as he reached out to cup her face with his hands. The salesman seemed to move in close to her and brush a kiss against her cheek.

Seth and Mark sat staring. Mark looked at Seth, who was stunned speechless. Seth could not comprehend the change in fortune. His disappointment quickly turned to anger. He felt embarrassed, assuming that he had surely been duped by April. He was disappointed with himself for letting his guard down. He wondered if he had somehow misjudged or misunderstood the entire situation.

Mark patted Seth on the shoulder, trying to console him.

"Sorry Seth," Mark said. "Women are strange."

Mark continued in vain with his words of encouragement. He was the sort of person who always looked at the bright side of any situation.

"At least you hadn't invested much into her," Mark said.

Seth didn't respond. He worried that Mark might be able to tell that he was on the verge of tears. Seth stared at April, watching as she conversed with the salesman.

10

The next morning, Seth worked at his dorm room desk while Mark concentrated on his football video game.

"Just let it go Seth," Mark said. "We all get burned from time to time. It's not doing you any good to dwell on it."

"I know," Seth said. He had been unsuccessfully trying to pour himself into his school work since waking up early. "I just can't believe it. It seemed I finally had something clicking and then it got ripped away from me."

"Huh," Mark said, still oblivious to the depth of Seth's misery. "So the truth comes out."

"What do you mean?" Seth asked.

"You did like that girl."

Seth took in a deep breath and turned to face Mark.

"Of course I did," Seth admitted.

Mark nodded. His demeanor was softer than it had been in the past. "Don't be so ashamed about it. Nobody's castrating you for admitting it."

"She already did a good enough job of that," Seth said.

"This doesn't have to be like that," Mark said.

"Well it is."

Seth was angry at himself for letting April distract him. He knew that his productivity would be harmed as he tried to forget about her. Above all, that was what he had feared all along.

"You were overdue to find a girl who you liked," Mark said. "If you were dating more often, it wouldn't hurt like this when things don't work out."

Seth was sharp in his response.

"What advice is that?" he said. "You've had the same

girlfriend for the past two years."

Mark was confused by Seth's argument. "What does that have to do with anything?"

"I'm just saying," Seth said. "Being told to play the field by someone who's been on the bench that long isn't very solid advice."

"Trust me," Mark said. "I played the field long and hard for years. You just don't remember what it's like to get shot down."

Seth knew that Mark meant well, but his advice wasn't the best for that particular moment.

"I'm having a hard time getting her out of my head," Seth said.

"That's what it is," Mark said. "All mental. Let me illustrate your problem."

Mark reached for a magazine and flipped through it. When he finally reached a specific page, he pointed to a sports car. It was profiled in a double-page spread.

Mark asked. "What is this?"

"It's a Ferrari." Seth said.

"Good," Mark said. "This is the fastest production car in the world and I want it badly. But I have a problem. Do you know what that is?

Seth had hoped that Mark might have something enlightening to say, but that did not seem to be the case. He grew disinterested by the exercise.

"I give up," Seth said.

Mark was insistent. "Make a guess."

"You have no money and no job?"

"Exactly," Mark said, pointing to the picture of the Ferrari again. "No matter how much I want this car, it isn't going to happen because there isn't any money in here."

Mark reached over to his desk for his wallet and opened it up. It was empty.

"Now," Mark continued. "You don't see me staring out of windows thinking about something that I can't have. Maybe you should stop thinking about things that you can't have."

Rather than feeling better about his state of affairs, Seth grew frustrated.

"You realize that had nothing to do with this situation,"

he said.

Before Mark could respond, there was a knock at the dorm room's entrance door. Mark stood up to answer it, but first added to Seth. "Just forget about her."

Mark then swung open the entry door to reveal April standing in the hallway. Mark and Seth both looked at her with shocked expressions.

"Hi," April said. "Can I talk to Seth?"

April did not wait for an answer before stepping into the room. Mark inched past her, heading out the door.

"Hey Seth," Mark said. "I'm going into town to get that, uh, thing."

Mark pulled the door shut. Seth faced April, instantly feeling the wall of invisible tension between them.

"Hello," April said.

"Hi." Seth said.

Seth was too angry and disappointed to say anything further. April kept the conversation going.

"Where did you run off to last night?" she asked. "When I came back, you'd left."

"I didn't think you needed me anymore." Seth said. "You and your boyfriend seemed to be doing fine together."

"Boyfriend?"

"Yeah. The guy who you were talking to. He kissed you."

April didn't seem to have any idea who Seth was talking about. She gave Seth a confused look before appearing to pull the pieces together.

"Bobby?" April asked. "He's just an old friend."

"Old friend?" Seth said.

April giggled at Seth's cold behavior. "And I wouldn't have let him kiss me."

"Okay," Seth said, not entirely sure what to believe. He replayed the events in his mind again, trying to understand how he might have been mistaken. Perhaps what he thought had been a kiss had not been. The lighting in the dance area had not been ideal.

"Look," April said. "I had a great time with you last night. At least, before you ran off. I wanted to get together again."

Seth was so surprised by her matter-of-fact statements that his eyes almost popped out of their sockets. He stammered.

"You're asking me on a date?"

"I guess that I am," April said. "Aren't I?"

Seth was speechless, but April continued to smile at him. He felt torn.

Given how badly Seth had felt all night and all morning, part of him had wished that somehow there remained a chance with April. Even in those moments though, he had never imagined such a dramatic reversal might occur.

By the same token, Seth was still not entirely sure if he could or should trust April. Taking a deep breath, Seth ultimately decided to take another chance on her.

"Okay," he said.

"How about tomorrow afternoon?" April said. "I have class until two, but I'm free after that."

Seth realized that he had a conflict. April was suggesting having a date on a Monday afternoon. It was not ideal timing, given his busy schedule.

"I have a lab later in the afternoon..." he said.

April looked disappointed. Seth could tell that, after his behavior the prior night, he needed to make something work.

"I can skip it," he said. "It's no big deal."

"Great," April said.

Seth smiled at April as she left his room.

11

The next day, Seth and April laced up their rented ice skates on a bench near a sheet of groomed ice. Families and couples skated around them on the large outdoor ice rink. Sparse clouds floated along in the blue sky overhead.

When planning the particulars of their date, Seth had assumed that they might simply go to a movie and have dinner. Then he remembered that the town of Winneshiek was a popular outdoor destination and he ran several ideas by April.

April had been the one to choose ice skating and, as was beginning to be the case with her, it was an unconventional choice. Seth and April were the only college students at the rink that afternoon.

Seth had not ice skated in years. His mother was a decent ice skater, going back to her own childhood, and she had tried to teach Seth those skills when he was younger. He had learned the basics back then and had not worn a pair of skates in over a decade.

"So," Seth said. "You'll show me some tricks right?"

"No," April said. "I didn't say that. I haven't been skating for years."

Seth breathed a sigh of relief.

"Come on," April said, shuffling in her skates toward the ice. "I'm not that rusty. You showed me how to dance, so I'm showing you how to skate."

April and Seth stepped onto the ice together. Seth felt uneasy as he tried to keep his balance.

"The only thing I'll be learning is how to get up off the ice." Seth said.

April scolded him.

"No Mr. Negatives allowed at this lesson," she said.

Seth was still unsure of his balance, so he reached onto the railing along the ring's perimeter. With that crutch, he slowly skated along.

In contrast, April warmed up by skating out into the open middle of the rink. She made two quick circles around the center of the rink, shaking off her rustiness. She then picked up speed and did a modest twirl. She stuttered on the landing but still seemed pleased with the result.

"Show-off!" Seth yelled over from his spot along the rink's perimeter.

"Don't get jealous," April said. She skated back over to Seth. "Let me help you."

April took Seth's hand and led him out onto the open ice, falling in behind a pack of people circling the rink.

"Don't think about falling down Seth," April said. "It's all mental."

"Yeah," Seth said. "Mental and ten years of practice."

Seth tried to relax and let his natural movements take over. He felt like he had to robotically will every movement of his legs. Unfortunately, he knew that was only making it harder.

"You're getting it," April said. "That's it, back and forth."

A little boy and little girl skated around the couple, teasing one another as they passed in front of Seth and April. The kids both looked back and giggled at Seth's struggles.

Seth was annoyed by their behavior. His cranky reaction caused April to continue laughing and smiling at him. Her demeanor had a therapeutic quality to it that made Seth relax. He calmed down and became more confident.

"This isn't so hard after all," Seth said. "When do we get to do some real tricks?"

After asking his question, Seth hit a rough patch of ice. He immediately dropped to the ground. It took April a moment to notice his absence behind her. She turned sharply to backtrack to Seth, where he was getting up onto his feet.

"I'm so sorry," April said, seeming horrified that Seth might have been injured. "Are you okay?"

"It's okay," Seth said. "I just got a little cocky, that's all. It's not your fault."

April looked concerned.

"Maybe we should do something else," she said. "This probably wasn't a great idea."

Seth considered the offer for a moment, but he did not want to give up already.

"No, let's keep trying," Seth said. He got a smirk on his face. "At least until I break something."

After skating together throughout the rest of the afternoon, Seth and April headed to an early dinner. Seth had suggested the dinner location, although there had not been much in the way of choices in Winneshiek. The town's dining options consisted of sports bars, a few fast food franchises, and a couple of cafes.

Seth and April spent much of the evening at one of the cafes on Winneshiek's main street. Through the window, the glowing streetlights twinkled in the darkness.

Empty plates from various parts of their meal were scattered across the table of their window booth. As a waitress cleared the table, Seth and April's conversation did not wind down. April had been sharing stories about her experiences while volunteering at a local food bank and soup kitchen.

"A cute old man dropped soup all over the floor," she said. "So while I was cleaning that up, I looked back. There he was taking handfuls of bread from one of the bins along the food line."

"What'd you do?" Seth asked.

"I ignored it."

Seth seemed surprised. "What about the other people?"

"The soup kitchen had extra bread that day." April said. "Normally I would've had to confront the guy though."

Seth sat back in his seat, pushing his last plate aside. Their waitress quickly scooped it up.

"What if you confront some guy and he flips out?" Seth asked.

"It happens." April said. "You deal with it."

"You deal with it?" Seth was surprised by how dismissive April was about potentially having a desperate man angry at her. "Living in a world like that seems so crazy."

"You don't think you'll ever have a confrontation with an angry patient?" April asked.

"I'm sure that I will," Seth said. "But the environment is pretty sterile. I'm in control there."

"We usually have it kept under control," April said. "There are times, though, when I've been scared."

Seth could not understand why someone like April would want to put herself in such uncomfortable positions. He had been cynical and naive in the past, assuming that the pretty girls always sought out careers that would allow them to use their looks to make things easier.

"So why keep doing it?" he asked. "Someone like you could make a lot of money in a safer career."

"I don't care about the money," April said.

Seth smiled at her comment.

"At some point," he said. "Everybody cares about the money."

"Money is essential," April said. "But only to a point. You don't need much to get by and still live comfortably."

Her comment surprised Seth.

"What about doing things with friends?" Seth asked.

"I knew going into social work would mean lots of work and little pay," April said.

"So why do it?" Seth asked.

"My mom was a social worker. She'd take me along sometimes. She cared about helping people. I do too. The way that some people live is just horrible."

"Yeah," Seth said. He realized that he had probably sounded aloof. Seth had grown up in a stable environment. His family had not been wealthy, but they had not been poor either. Seth had not experienced the poverty that certainly existed around him, but was aware of it.

"People wouldn't believe it if they saw how some coke addicts live," April said. "Needles lying around. Kids playing with paraphernalia."

"Geez," Seth said, taken aback by the instant imagery that flashed into his head.

"We'd move the kids out," April said. "At least until the parents had been through rehab. My mom was determined to help them make their lives better and avoid getting caught up in cycles."

"You're following in her footsteps?"

"In a way," April said. "It's about helping people. Not every job like that will make you as wealthy as a doctor.

The tide shifted when Seth realized that she was pushing at him. Testing him.

"Oh come on." Seth said. "The money might be there, but who knows when I'll ever have time to enjoy it."

"What is it then?" April asked. "I've spilled my guts. You can spill yours."

Seth instinctively tensed up.

"It's not a very simple answer," he said.

April flashed a smile and sat back, as though she were 'getting comfortable.'

"I've got plenty of time to hear it," she said.

"Well," Seth started. He hesitated before continuing. "I was sixteen and my dad found out that he was going to die from a brain tumor."

April gasped, embarrassed that she had made light of his choice in her setup.

"I'm sorry," she said. "I shouldn't have..."

"It's okay," Seth said. "It was a long time ago. Good things have come out of it."

"What kinds of things?"

"If the doctors hadn't cared, my father would've died in a lot of pain."

"What'd they do?"

Seth glanced down at their empty table.

"They made every effort to make sure that he died in peace," Seth said. "They didn't give up on him, even though they knew that they couldn't help him."

Seth looked up at April.

"A few hours before he died," Seth said. "I spent some time alone with my dad. He told me that he hoped I could someday help people like the doctors had helped him."

Seth turned away from April's gaze and looked out at the streetlights that were illuminating the downtown. He did not usually have difficulty discussing those events with family, but he had never discussed them much with his friends.

"That's why you're going to medical school?" April asked.

"Yeah," Seth said.

April seemed to think about Seth's statement for a moment, but she did not pry further into it.

"Our career paths aren't that different," she said. "In the end we both want to help people."

"Yeah," Seth said. "I keep them alive."

April's mouth twisted into a smile.

"And I keep them living," she said.

12

After Seth's date with April, he headed back to his dorm room to retrieve his backpack. Despite the time already being late, he had planned to catch up on his studies that night at the library. Being a Monday evening, it was still a 'school night.'

When Seth entered the room, he found Mark, as usual, playing a video game.

"The contender has returned," Mark said. "Do we have a new champion?"

Seth tried to act annoyed at first, but he could not suppress a smile from appearing on his face. He knew that the night had gone well, so he couldn't hide his happiness.

"Ladies and Gentlemen," Mark said. "We do indeed have a new champion!"

Mark held his hand up, expecting to receive a high-five. Seth half-heartedly complied.

"I need more," Mark said.

"You're not getting any more," Seth said.

Mark pressed. "Did you two..."

Seth guffawed. "Of course not."

"Okay, don't panic," Mark said. "Did you give her a nice kiss goodnight?"

"No," Seth said. "The moment never felt quite right."

Mark slapped his hands on his knees.

"It doesn't have to!" he said.

Seth pulled several of his textbooks off of his shelf and put them into his backpack.

"You wanted me to force myself on her?" Seth asked.

"No man," Mark said. "We're gentlemen."

"I might be," Seth said. "I'm not sure about the rest of you guys."

"Let me ask you, did she laugh?"

"Usually."

"That's great."

Seth corrected Mark. "Usually because I had done something to look like an idiot,"

"It doesn't matter," Mark said. "You're in."

"What're you talking about? Seth said.

"You're in," Mark said. "You made her laugh. You make any woman laugh and you're already halfway there."

Seth zipped up his backpack and headed back out of his dorm room. On his way out, he turned back to Mark.

"Already where?" he asked. "You're talking gibberish."

"There man," Mark said. "There."

2:
Winter

13

Seth's next date with April was more low-key than their first. It was later in the week and Seth was studying for a quiz that was scheduled for the next morning, but he had suggested they go for a walk into Winneshiek as a break.

The nighttime in Winneshiek had a certain magical quality to it. The downtown looked majestic with its streetlights and store signs glowing. Snow was lightly falling on the sidewalk as April and Seth made slow strides through the low drifts. With most of the town's residents having retired into their homes earlier that evening, Seth and April enjoyed the peaceful conditions.

"We should go sledding on Saturday," Seth said. "I haven't done that since I was a kid."

"What did you have in mind?" April asked.

"I'm not sure yet. There are a couple of ski slopes on the edge of town that we could probably use. They might be fun to try if they were deserted. They're not usually open for skiing anyway."

April took a moment to respond to the suggestion.

"Last year," she said. "When it was snowing, I headed over there to sled with Bobby and his friends. We were chased by the police through the woods for trespassing."

"Oh really?"

"Yeah, it was a long night. We ended up hiking to the top of a bluff in the dark. There weren't any trails, so we walked through the snow-covered brush and frozen ravines. It should have been a warning that he wasn't my kind of guy."

Seth was confused by April's last remark.

"I thought you never dated Bobby?" he asked.

"No," April said. "I did. A while ago."

Seth was taken aback by April's admission. In the back of his mind, he could have sworn that Bobby had been only referred to as an 'old friend.' As Seth's relationship with April was still so new, they had not spent much time discussing past relationships.

Against his better judgment, Seth let his curiosity get the better of him.

"Well," he said. "When did you break up?"

"Three months ago in December," April said.

"Wait," Seth said. "So two months ago?"

April sighed. It was obvious that she didn't want to discuss Bobby, but Seth disregarded her discomfort. He was too curious to know better.

"If you need to be technical," she said. "Now he's just a friend."

"A good friend?"

"Better than some," April said, catching herself. "We're not close anymore though."

Seth was confused by April's statement.

"Isn't that a bit cryptic?" he asked.

"It's just that I don't care to dwell on my ex-boyfriends," April said. "That's in the past."

The tension that April was radiating was finally noticed by Seth. He decided to let things go for the time being.

"I guess." he said.

"Besides," April said. "Isn't it bad luck or something to talk about past relationships on a date?"

Seth tried to sound serious. "You mean this is a date?"

April seemed caught off guard by the remark, unsure if Seth was joking or not. Finally, Seth smiled to reassure her.

"Just so that you know," Seth said. "I don't have any problem talking about my past relationships."

"And why's that?"

"There isn't much to say."

April cleared a light blanket of new snow off of a bench for the couple to sit on. Seth realized that she might be able to get payback for his interrogation of her a few moments earlier.

"You haven't dated anyone recently?" April asked.

"I was dating a girl after high school," Seth said. "We

broke up a few weeks after starting college. I haven't really dated much since then."

April added a dramatic tone to her reply. "The ever-popular doomed high school romance."

"I guess it happens to everybody," Seth said. "One day we found ourselves on two different paths."

"What's stopped you since then?"

"School," Seth said. "I needed to keep my grades up. That meant no free time. No free time meant no girlfriend."

April looked at her watch.

"You didn't have any problem taking this evening off," she said.

Seth was reminded that they had been out together much longer than he had realized. April had probably hit on a good point.

"I happened to have some time open up," Seth said, trying not to think about all of the work that would be waiting for him back on campus.

"Lucky me," April said.

"Yes," Seth said. "Lucky you."

14

While most of Seth's professors might not have taken notice of any decrease in his performance, he had been cognizant of a sudden dip in his productivity. While he had not spent much actual time with April over the course of the several days since their initial dates, he had spent massive amounts of time thinking about her.

Nevertheless, he had never been happier.

Seth had started to become comfortable with the idea of having a relationship. Previously, it had been virtually unheard of that he would take time away from studying on a Saturday afternoon. He did just that though the next weekend, taking a break from his studies to meet up with April in front of the campus library.

Park College's library sat to one side of the campus, separated from the student union building by a vast lawn. Given the recent snowfall, students were not able to sit on the grass like they often did in the spring or fall. However, Frisbee games still continued.

In one corner of the lawn, the snow was undisturbed, except for a few footprints that belonged to Seth and April. They were both bundled up for the colder weather, but Seth found himself overheating from his work efforts. Behind him, there was a long, empty strip of powder missing on the ground. Seth pushed as hard as he could against a big ball of wet snow. When he was ultimately satisfied by its size, he stopped.

"Now," Seth said. "What we need is..."

Before he could finish, Seth was hit in the back of the head by a large snowball. He turned around to catch April still snickering.

The blow stung enough that Seth paused to rub his head. April's expression immediately changed after she realized that he had been hurt.

"Are you okay?" she asked. "I'm sorry. I didn't mean to hit your head."

"I'm fine," Seth said. "It wasn't your fault."

April was close to Seth, touching the back of his head. They stopped for a moment. There was an unspoken acknowledgement that came and went in a fleeting instant.

The chemistry between them was apparent to Seth, but he had still not worked up the nerve to kiss April. They had held hands and hugged, so he had certainly had his opportunities, but he kept holding back.

Seth wanted their 'moment' to be memorable and let his knack for planning get the better of him. No moment ever seemed right or perfect and, as a result, nothing occurred. As several dates had gone by, he grew worried that April might even lose interest in him over his hesitations.

Seth finally broke the tension.

"We've got to get a body on this snowman," he said.

It was not much longer until they had completed the snowman by placing two proportionately smaller balls of snow on top of the base. April glanced at it, unsure.

"Did you forget something?" April asked.

"No," Seth said. "It looks finished."

Seth examined the snowman before a realization came to mind. "We forgot to bring a nose."

He turned to April in disappointment, but she perked up, and had a sly smile on her face.

"No," April said. "You forgot to bring a nose."

April reached into her coat and pulled out a long, slender carrot. Seth was amused.

"You always carry one of those around?" he asked.

That evening, the stars shone brightly. One advantage of Park College's rather remote location in Winneshiek was a low level of light pollution. As a result, a clear night sky often looked incredible.

Two shadows moved together toward the middle of the campus football field. Seth and April were the only two people in the area that evening.

"Remind me," he said. "Who signs up for a class that requires lab work outside in the winter?"

"It isn't that bad out," April said, looking comfortable in her cold-weather attire. "Besides, I need help with my Astronomy lab. You know, from the class that you got an 'A' in last semester. That sounds like as good of a tutor as I've ever heard."

Seth was cold. He did not understand how April could be so comfortable in the cold.

"But you've said that I study too much and look at this," Seth said as he pulled a pair of binoculars out of his pocket. "Here we are doing school work on a Saturday night."

"It's been cloudy at night all week," April said. "Who knows when we'll get another night like this one. Besides, you'll get to watch a movie with me later. We'll warm up together."

"Let's hurry then," Seth said. He was not oblivious to the invitation and his mind started racing. As usual, he began overthinking what might be ahead for them that evening. He grew anxious about finally kissing her.

April leafed through a small notebook.

"First up," she said. "Andromeda."

"That's easy," Seth said, pointing over at a star to the north. "It's the bright one right there to the north."

April looked up and then back down from her notebook, making notes in the process.

"I see it," she said. "That wasn't a problem. How about Pisces?"

"That's more difficult to find," Seth said. "Tilt your head as far back as you can."

Seth and April huddled next to each other. April had her head tilted back while Seth stood over her. He handed her his binoculars and helped guide her view.

"It's right above Andromeda," Seth said. "But you'll need to look for the groupings of stars."

"I don't see it."

"Move your head more this way."

Seth pulled his warm hands out of his pockets and placed them on April's bare face. He gently shifted her head to one side.

The frustration drained from April's face as she forgot about the stars and turned her attention to Seth.

Both of their eyes met. Finally, for once, Seth knew that it was time to move forward. It ended up being a perfect moment, but it had only become one because it had been unplanned. At least, Seth thought that it had been unplanned.

They kissed.

An instant later, their lips parted.

"Maybe it's not so cold out here," Seth said.

Seth and April both laughed, their foggy breath swirling up between them. They kissed again, this time much longer.

15

Later the next week, Seth stood nervously outside of Professor Lee's office. He could see the back of Lee's head from through a crack in the door's stained glass. When Seth finally worked up the nerve, he knocked at the door.

"Yes," Professor Lee said, his voice projecting loudly from inside the office. "Come in."

Seth opened the office door, walked into the room, and took a seat next to Lee's desk. The office was small and cluttered with piles of books. Seth often wondered if the levels of shelving that lined the walls might someday collapse under the weight of so many large reference tomes.

Professor Lee stayed at his computer, keeping his back to Seth. When he next spoke, the tone in his voice intimidated Seth. "Do you know why I called you here?"

"No Professor Lee." Seth answered. He had assumed that it was probably not for something positive.

"Your Organic Chemistry instructor, Professor Larson, came to speak with me."

Seth instantly became worried. Although Larson's office was just down a hallway from Lee, there were few reasons that the pair would speak about a student.

"Why?" Seth asked.

"You took a test from him recently," Lee said.

Seth thought back to one of his many recent exams. "We had a test a couple of days ago."

"How do you think that you did?"

Seth tried to guess positively. "It went okay."

Professor Lee spun around, holding the test in his hand. It

was covered with red marks.

"You received a 'C'-level grade," Lee said.

Seth was so surprised by the results of the test that he blurted out his reply. "Are you serious?"

"Look for yourself," Lee said, handing Seth the test.

Seth was dumbfounded and kept staring at the red marks on the test with dismay.

"I can't believe this," he said.

"I can't either," Professor Lee said. "Until this instance, you had an 'A' on every other exam. Can you tell me how this occurred?"

"I don't…" Seth said. "I don't know what to say."

"You realize the seriousness," Lee said. "Don't you? Organic Chemistry is a make or break class for any aspiring medical student."

Seth was reeling as the gravity of the test score hit him.

"I realize that," Seth said. "I just don't think that I can offer an explanation right now."

Professor Lee was annoyed by Seth's reluctance.

"Really?" Lee asked, seeming surprised. "Seth, as your advisor, you know that you can come to me with any problems."

"I know," Seth said.

"Is there something distracting you?" Lee asked. "Can I do anything to help?"

Seth could tell that Lee seemed disappointed, but not just with the test results. Seth's reluctance to explain what might have happened was odd and would only further worry Lee.

Seth was tempted to mention his new relationship with April and how that had been causing him distractions from his studies. He feared that such a confession might only bring further scorn from Lee, so Seth kept it to himself.

"I can't think of anything," he said.

Lee sighed and looked Seth in the eyes.

"The faculty is always here for our students," he said. "If you need help, come to any of us. This is not the time to drop the ball."

Lee's last words hung over Seth and made him feel guilty.

"I won't sir," he said. "I've worked too hard to fall short."

"Good," Lee said. "Remember how hard you've worked when things are difficult and that will give you focus."

16

Seth's meeting with Professor Lee had occurred immediately prior to Park College's Thanksgiving break. Literally hours later, both Seth and April had returned to their respective homes to spend the holiday with family.

Their relationship was still new. While it seemed increasingly defined, Seth had not felt comfortable bringing it up to relatives whom he encountered during the holiday. He spoke with April on the telephone while also exchanging text messages and emails.

Seth had been reluctant to share his recent organic chemistry struggles with April, thinking that she might see it as a reason to 'cool' things between them. It was an irrational thought, but he let it linger. After a few days of keeping things hidden, Seth decided that he needed to get his head back in order and finally shared the news with April.

Upon learning about Seth's struggles, April was supportive of not letting their relationship cause his academics to slide. She didn't suggest a break, but she did come up with ideas to help Seth. During the first week after returning to campus, their time together was spent with more efficiency in mind.

As a result, other aspects of Seth's social life took on a smaller role. It was not until later in that first post-break week that Seth was able to spend significant time with his friends. He had barely seen Dave or Tony since before the Thanksgiving break and he had only spoken with Mark in passing in their room.

Seth made firm plans to meet with his friends later in the week. After finishing a late afternoon class, he walked from campus down to the Philadelphia Bar and Grill. It was an eatery that his friends often frequented when they were not interested in the cafeteria menu. Like most restaurants in Winneshiek, the food was remarkably inexpensive. Thus, it was popular with students.

After Seth arrived, he settled into a booth with Dave and Tony. They were already in mid-conversation.

"So I was dancing all night with this girl," Tony said. "We were grinding. It was all hot and sweaty."

"The whole night?" Dave said.

Tony picked at his food, trying to build up the drama for Dave.

"Until closing," he said. "Then I walked out of the place."

"She followed you?" Dave asked.

"Oh yeah," Tony said.

Dave fed right into Tony's baiting. He was eager to know what had happened next. "You went back to your place?"

Tony let the question linger before responding.

"No," he said. "Her place. Her roommate was out of town."

Dave edged up close to Tony.

"So you stayed over?" Dave asked.

Tony sat back and put his hands behind his head.

"Gentlemen," Tony said. "I showed her a new world she'd never known existed."

Dave kept feeding Tony leading questions. "What happened in the morning?"

"I woke up," Tony said. "At which point you know how she was cooing all over me."

"Of course," Dave said.

"Well," Tony said. "Then the crazy part happened. We headed outside. As I was walking to my car, I turned back to her and said 'Thanks for the great night Amy, I'll call you later.'"

Dave looked disappointed. He wasn't sure why Tony had brought up the story if it did not end in dramatic fashion.

"What's so crazy about that?" Dave asked.

"The problem was," Tony said, taking a deep breath before revealing a smirk. "Her name wasn't Amy. I'd screwed up her name. She started crying."

"That sucks," Dave said, suddenly interested again.

"It got worse," Tony said. "She yelled over 'My name's

Annie you creep.'"

"Oh no," Dave said.

"So I was trying to save it," Tony said. "I yell back 'Amy, Annie, it doesn't matter, you're my baby.'"

Dave laughed in disbelief.

"That worked?" he asked.

"No," Tony said, shaking his head. "Of course not. She went psycho. You know that big dent in my hood?"

"No way," Dave said.

"Yeah," Tony said. "She put that in my car. She was so mad that I didn't know what to do. I was yelling, screaming."

Dave's demeanor became serious.

"Exactly the point I was making," he said, seemingly referring to a discussion that had taken place before Seth had arrived. "Guys get a raw deal in the morning."

Tony and Dave glanced over at Seth. By that point, he had started reading a stray newspaper that was at their table.

"Hey Seth," Tony said. "You ever call April the wrong name?"

Seth looked up from the newspaper.

"It's times like this when I wonder why I hang out with you guys," Seth said.

Both Dave and Tony looked wounded by Seth's statement.

"Don't forget who loves you," Tony said.

"Stop changing the subject Seth," Dave said. "You and Miss Jordan have a fight?"

"No," Seth said.

Seth's food arrived and he began nibbling at his fries.

"It's just that I'm surprised that you're out with us and not with her," Dave said. "This is the first time we've had dinner with you since we got back from break."

"I've just been trying to juggle everything," Seth said. "April's working on a group project tonight and I'll be up late finishing a lab."

"I figured that you didn't have time for us anymore," Tony said. "With all your scoring."

"Not really," Seth said.

"What does that mean?" Dave asked, clearly confused. "Not really?"

"It means that in over a month with her," Tony said. "He

hasn't gotten anywhere."

Seth knew better than to take Tony's bait, but he could not resist responding.

"That's not what I said," he said.

"Excuses," Tony said. "Dave, if there was anything happening, this man would be spilling it."

Seth tried to take the high road out of the conversation. "I don't feel like talking to the loveline."

Dave looked at his beer. His mood became surprisingly somber.

"I can't believe that you've been with her for so long," Dave said. "I can't even remember the last time that I had a date."

"We've only been dating for like three weeks," Seth said. "And during part of that time, we were all on break."

Dave took no consolation in Seth's clarifications.

"The next thing you know," he said. "It'll be December, then second semester."

"Dave," Seth said. "It is December."

Dave slammed his hand down on the table.

"No way!" he yelled.

Dave's random mood changes continued.

"Guys," Dave said. "I could go for some weed right now."

Seth was surprised at the bluntness of Dave's statement. It helped explain why Dave might be speaking erratically.

"I thought that you had quit." Seth said.

"A man can still be weak once in a while can't he?" Dave asked, looking for sympathy.

Tony offered a solution. "You can get some from Gene at Cowboy's."

Seth knew that he should not have been surprised that Tony would have such connections, but he was.

Tony caught a glimpse of Seth's startled reaction and smiled at him.

"Maybe we'll run into your girlfriend over there Seth," Tony said.

"I doubt it." Seth said.

Seth knew that April was spending the evening working on a group project for one of her classes. However, Tony's unusual smirk still made Seth feel uncomfortable. Whenever Tony had that look on his face, things often did not seem to work in Seth's favor.

"Oh," Tony said. "I see her there with her little posse. At least, I used to see here there once in a while."

Seth knew that Tony would be seeking a reaction, so he tried not to give him one. In Seth's moments of insecurity, he stressed over the fact that April had led a much more outgoing life around campus. For that reason, he assumed that she might eventually get bored with him.

"Really," he said.

"You ever been to Cowboy's?" Tony asked Seth.

"No," Seth replied.

"Maybe you should check it out," Tony said. "You might like it. Your girlfriend did."

17

The last thing that Seth had imagined spending his evening doing was going to another bar. Unfortunately, Tony's statements about April being a regular at Cowboy's had made him curious and he found himself heading there with his friends.

As Seth, Dave, and Tony made their way through the run-down entrance into Cowboy's, Seth immediately disliked what he encountered. The main bar area sat near the entrance and was crowded. The rest of the room was also packed with customers. Despite an official smoking ban across businesses in Winneshiek, a cloud of smoke from customers' cigarettes hung in the air. The other side of the bar's interior was divided by a low wall with tables and chairs strewn around the room.

The customers were crowded around the tables and bar or stood in clusters near both. Seth was surprised by the diversity of the customers. Most of them appeared to be 'townies,' a term that the students used when referring to the local residents of Winneshiek.

Typically, the townies and the students did not hang out at the same bars. In fact, Seth heard stories from students who had ventured off of the beaten path to a townie bar. Before long, they were made to feel unwelcome in such establishments. Usually it meant annoyed looks from the townie patrons, but sometimes actual words of insult were exchanged.

Such segregation was not, apparently, the case at Cowboy's. Young and old, college students and locals, Cowboy's brought them all together.

As Seth and his friends took seats in the rear of the serving area, Seth was struck by the jovial chaos of the scene. He knew that he didn't fit in there; a feeling was made more certain when his smoke allergy acted up. The desire to return to his studies gnawed at him. For all express purposes, Seth looked and acted like a tourist at the bar.

"Isn't this place great?" Tony asked Seth.

Seth continued to find nothing at all impressive about Cowboy's.

"I think that my foot just stuck to something on the floor," he said. "This is where you go every week?"

Seth had not bothered to try to hide the disdain in his voice. Tony did not react well to the remark.

"Don't question the methods of the man Sethy," Tony said.

Dave looked around at the crowd as though he was searching for someone.

"Gene's not here," Dave said, looking to Tony for answers. "Now who do I get the weed from?"

No one seemed to care about Dave's plight.

"I don't see April around here anywhere," Tony said.

"I didn't suppose that we would," Seth said.

"Maybe she'll stop in later."

His curiosity satisfied, Seth continued thinking about how he would extract himself from the situation. He was not entirely comfortable leaving his friends, knowing that they had been drinking at the restaurant and would likely continue to drink at Cowboy's. He knew that Tony's car was parked nearby and felt a certain obligation to drive them back to campus. Just the same, he didn't want to sit out with them all night.

Seth pushed his chair back, readying to stand up. "Look guys, I should get back to campus. Did you want me to drive you back?"

Neither Dave nor Tony bothered to respond to Seth's question. Tony also continued to avoid Dave's questions about alternative drug dealers and Dave grew frustrated with him. Amid that annoyance, Dave motioned for Seth to wait and then turned to Tony.

"So are you going to tell him the story," Dave said. "Or do I have to?"

Tony looked surprisingly uncomfortable by the question.

"I don't think that we need to bring it up," he said.

"What story?" Seth asked.

"The one about Tony hitting on April a few months back," Dave said, pointing to a corner near the bar. "Right over by the jukebox."

Seth settled back into his chair. He found it strange that Tony had not mentioned such an incident during their prior conversations about April. Tony was prideful though and, presumably, the story would reveal a hit to his pride.

"Oh really?" Seth said. For once, Seth felt as though he had the upper hand in a conversation.

"Yeah," Dave said. "What was it that you said to her again? Oh yeah, he marched over and said 'I must have just died.'"

Tony stopped paying attention to the conversation and glanced over at the bar.

"Why would he say that?" Seth asked.

"That's what she asked him," Dave said. "So he says 'You're an angel and angels are only in heaven.' She just walked away like he was the biggest idiot on the planet. She didn't even say a word."

Dave bent over laughing. He touched Tony's shoulder to get his attention.

"What movie did you rip that line off from?" Dave asked.

Clearly humiliated, Tony neither acknowledged the question nor look at Seth. He tried to change the subject.

"Look at the honeys over at the bar," Tony said.

Seth and Dave both looked over at two girls sitting together at the bar. They were modestly attractive, but a little trashy looking.

"That's the most beautiful woman I've ever seen," Tony said, with full sincerity.

"Her friend isn't bad either," Dave said. "Big hair, but what can you do?"

Tony stood up and motioned to Dave. "Let's get to work compadre."

Dave rose to follow Tony toward the bar.

"Where are you guys going?" Seth asked.

"I've got to work buddy," Tony said. "Just be a minute."

Seth watched the pair approach the women at the bar and knew that it would be much longer than a minute. In his mind,

Seth continued to debate the pros and cons of walking back to campus and leaving his friends on their own. Ultimately, Seth decided to stay for a few more minutes. To pass the time, he walked over to a booming jukebox.

There were several crowded tables situated around the jukebox, but Seth found himself alone at the machine. He flipped through the song choices, feeling uncomfortable. He was surrounded by the many nearby townies who seemed to be sizing him up. As Seth was about to drop money into the machine, he heard a woman's voice from behind his head.

"Hey kid!" the woman said.

Seth whipped around. He found himself facing a middle-aged biker-type, dressed in black leather. She was sitting on the lap of a burly man who also looked like a biker.

The woman continued. "What do you think you're doing?"

"I'm playing a song," Seth said.

"That's my machine," the woman said. "I'm the one who decides what music gets played."

The biker, whose lap the woman was sitting on, piped up.

"Listen to the lady kid," he said. "Go sit down. I don't think that you want to cause any trouble."

"Sorry," Seth said. "I didn't mean anything. I'm not from around here."

"That a fact?" the other biker asked.

Tony rescued Seth by pulling him aside. He had been entirely oblivious to Seth's prior predicament.

"Listen," Tony said. "These women want us."

Seth didn't care.

"I need to get going," he said.

Tony took a long pause before pleading. "But they want us bad."

Seth looked back at the bar, in the direction of the women. He watched Dave throw down a drink while one of the girls laughed and pounded on his chest.

"What am I supposed to do?" Seth asked.

Tony handed him a set of keys.

"Take my car back," Tony said. "I'm sure we'll be getting a ride back with the ladies."

Tony returned to the bar. Turning around, he gave Seth

an enthusiastic thumbs-up.

Seth took the car keys in his hand and walked out of the bar.

18

Seth and April were together the next day, soon after classes had completed for the week. They had both agreed that it would be fun to work out and met at the campus recreation center.

Most students were making plans for dinner or evening trips away from Winneshiek. As a result, Seth and April entered a recreation area with several basketball courts and found that they had the space entirely to themselves.

"I never thought that my group was going to get done practicing last night," April said. "We were up until after two in the morning."

"How did that presentation go?" Seth asked.

"It was fine," April said. "I think. What'd you do?"

"It was pretty lame," Seth said.

April's curiosity was raised.

"Why was that?" she asked.

"I went out to dinner with Dave and Tony," Seth said. "Then we went to Cowboy's Bar. I don't know if it's your kind of place. It wasn't mine."

"Oh," April said. "I've been there."

Seth's heart sank. He had assumed that he had started figuring out what kind of person April was. He had a hard time reconciling the reassuringly innocent image that he'd constructed with the atmosphere that he had experienced at Cowboy's

"Really?" he asked. "What'd you think of it?"

"It used to be cool," April said. "Things have sort of changed there though."

"Like what?"

April thought about it for a moment before continuing. "Maybe it was me."

"You liked the people there?" Seth asked.

"Most of them," April said. "Once in a while some old guy would hit on me, but otherwise they were okay."

"What'd you do if that happened?" Seth asked.

"Well," April said. "If he was rich or cute, I'd go home with him. A young girl is usually powerless in the presence of an older man."

"That's not funny," Seth said. "It just seemed like a rough place."

April looked around for a basketball, seeming disinterested in the topic.

"Don't get all weird about it Seth," she said. "I can take care of myself."

Seth began to apologize. "Sorry, I didn't mean to..."

April cut Seth off by grabbing a basketball and started to dribble toward him.

"Don't worry about it," she said. "Worry about me."

Seth perked up as April tried to run by him. Seth and April were quickly facing off, one on one. April guarded the ball against Seth, but he was eventually able to steal it from her.

With the ball in his control, Seth made his move. It was a fast juke toward the basket, but April was quicker. After a flurry of movement between the pair, April stole the ball back. Seth tried to defend against her, but tripped over himself and landed on the hardwood flooring.

With his chin resting against the polished wood surface, Seth watched as April jumped up and threw the ball into the hoop. Two points in her favor.

April looked back, finally noticing that Seth had fallen. She looked concerned, but Seth waved it off.

As Seth stood back onto his feet, he yelled over to April in mock defeat. "There are subtler ways of proving a point."

After finishing their game and having dinner at the campus's student run cafe, Seth and April readied for a party. April had been invited to the party by people whom she had described as 'old friends' and Seth had agreed that they should attend. Not being a partier, Seth had not been interested in attending, but it seemed of interest to April.

By the time both were ready to head out, dusk had long past and it had become chilly outside. Nonetheless, April had suggested that they walk over to the party's location, which was several blocks from campus. Despite the cold temperature, it was a lovely evening for a stroll. April and Seth walked next to one another down the sidewalk of a darkened residential street.

"You never told me," April said. "Did you get started dissecting that body?"

"His name's Frank," Seth said.

April's tone betrayed her disgust.

"Sorry," April said. "Did you get to cut Frank open today?"

"Actually," Seth said. "Professor Lee had me demonstrate with him for the class. Everyone else had to wait until Monday."

"That's quite an honor," April said, sounding impressed.

Seth brushed her comment aside.

"Are you trying to make me cocky?" Seth asked

"You can be cocky around me," April said. "You shouldn't be ashamed of being the smartest person in the department."

"I'm not ashamed," Seth said. "It's just…"

Seth's train of thought was interrupted by the sound of hard rock music. He realized that he could likely hear the party in the distance.

"Is that the party?" Seth asked.

"Maybe," April said.

Seth pulled April close, putting his hands around her waist.

"Are you sure that you want to go?" Seth asked.

April giggled as Seth moved in to kiss her, but she stopped him.

"Patience tiger," April said.

Seth was frustrated but reacted in a playful manner.

"Maybe I won't be in the mood later," he said.

"I'm sorry," April said, checking her watch. "But we're already late."

The pair resumed their walk.

"You remember my friend Susan?" April asked

"The one with that boyfriend," Seth said. "Barry?"

"Right. His parents were up last weekend and the whole time Barry kept calling her his 'friend' Susan."

"Never his 'girlfriend?'"

"Not once."

Seth seemed surprised by the slight.

"They've been dating quite a while haven't they?" he asked.

"Six weeks," April said. "It shouldn't have been difficult for him."

Seth and April strolled around the corner of the block. From their new vantage point, they could see a massive house-party in the distance. Music blared from it at a painful level. Empty bottles were strewn around the front lawn. Everyone who Seth could see outside were holding up beers and yelling to those approaching in the distance.

"Well," Seth said. "Next weekend, when my parents are visiting, they will be meeting my girlfriend."

April toyed with the comment, confident in it.

"So who's the lucky girl?" she asked.

"I'm not sure yet," Seth said. "I'm hoping to find her at the party."

"I'll try to help you out," April said.

"Oh," Seth said. "I know that you will."

Seth and April made their way through the party house's front door. After squeezing by throngs of people at the bottom of a staircase, they ended up in line to pay for their 'cups.'

The red plastic party cups being distributed would essentially allow them access to the house and any beer that they might have wanted to drink.

A stereotypical frat guy passed out the cups to a pair of sorority girls who had arrived ahead of Seth and April. The frat guy growled out a sloppy greeting to the girls. "Five bucks a cup."

"But we'll share it," the first sorority girl said.

"We're not drinking that much," the other sorority girl insisted.

"It's one cup per person," the frat guy said. "Pay or get out of here."

The girls grumbled to one another before both finally paid

their money. Each then received a cup. The frat guy next looked over at Seth.

"You need one buddy?" the frat guy asked.

"Two please," Seth said.

Seth handed over his money and, after receiving both cups, passed one to April.

"Thanks," April said. "Let's head upstairs, I bet it'll be less crowded."

Seth and April climbed the house's main staircase. Upon reaching the next level, they didn't find the upstairs any less packed. They pushed their way down the hallway until a college student, who struck Seth as a 'hippie-wannabe,' came out of one of the bedrooms. He instantly recognized April.

"April!" the hippie-wannabe said.

The hippie-wannabe pulled on April's arm, tugging her into the room that he had just exited. Based on a faint odor in the air, coupled with an erratic behavior, Seth assumed that the hippie-wannabe was under the influence of something.

After getting pulled partway into the bedroom, April stopped to introduce the hippe-wannabe to Seth.

"Kevin," she said. "This is Seth."

"Hi," Kevin said. He then ignored Seth, turning back to April. "You've got to say 'Hi' to Ilsa."

April looked surprised and motioned a confused Seth to follow her. Seth entered the bedroom and surveyed the scene. He noticed several other students strewn about, laughing and talking in drunken merriment.

April turned her head back to Seth and spoke barely loud enough for him to hear. "I haven't seen these guys in a while."

"I'm sure she'll be out in a minute," Kevin said, motioning to a closed closet door on the other side of the bedroom.

Somewhat randomly, or, as Seth presumed, due to being chemically altered, Kevin added. "That closet is so big inside."

Seth was not able to make much sense of the statement. He looked to April for answers, but she did not offer any.

"It's so great to see you April," Kevin said. "Where have you been this past month?"

"Things keep coming up," April said. "You know how it can be."

"So," Kevin said, leaning in close to April's ear. "Who's the stiff?"

April laughed at the question. Seth thought that she might have been trying to hide her embarrassment.

"Kevin," April said. "I just introduced you to him. This is Seth."

Kevin offered no apology. Instead, he reached out to shake Seth's hand. Kevin's balance teetered in the process.

"Kevin Lomax," he said. "Nice to meet you. How long have you guys been together?"

Seth looked at April, wondering if she would answer on his behalf. She did not, so he finally said. "A little over a month."

Kevin gave Seth an off-balance poke.

"Lucky man," he said. "Every guy at this place is jealous of you."

"Thanks," Seth said, feeling uncomfortable.

The bedroom's closet door opened. Thin clouds of smoke heralded people as they staggered out from inside. Those who emerged were, similarly to Kevin, loud. Their motions were sporadic.

"About time they let others in there," Kevin said to Seth.

Seth could tell that April seemed increasingly uncomfortable, but he was not entirely sure why.

"I need to use the ladies room," April said. "I'll be back in a minute."

April stepped around Seth, who continued to grow annoyed by what he observed around him. Kevin took a step closer to Seth.

"You need a smoke?" Kevin asked, somewhat to Seth's surprise. "We've got plenty in there."

"No thanks," Seth said.

"Don't worry man," Kevin said. "Any friend of April's gets a free smoke from me."

Much like he had felt at Cowboy's, Seth could not understand why April had apparently hung out with these people in the past. As he thought more about it, his level of annoyance and discomfort steadily grew.

"That's okay," Seth said. "Maybe some other time."

Seth looked through the haze of people still emerging from the closet and spotted Bobby, the suit salesman.

"I don't believe this," Seth said to himself.

Bobby noticed Seth and staggered over to him.

"Don't let her hurt you kid," Bobby said. "She'll bite if you make her mad."

Seth was too put off to respond. Bobby wandered out into the hallway and disappeared. The strange scene surrounding Seth had only become increasingly bizarre.

April returned to Seth's side an instant later. As the last of those from the closet then passed by Seth and April, April greeted several of them by name.

"Do you mind if we stay for a bit?" April said.

Seth withheld his complete dislike of the idea. "No, that's fine."

"I haven't seen a lot of these people in a while," April said. "I should say hello."

April led Seth over to a bed that was crowded with people seated around its perimeter. Seth turned to see a new group heading into the closet. Two students among that group squabbled with one another.

"Keep Brian away from the good stuff this time," one of the students said. "He's always hogging it."

"That's my stuff man," the other student said. He was, presumably, Brian. "I'll smoke it all night if I want."

Seth turned his head away and settled in on the edge of the mattress.

19

The day after the party, Seth met Dave at the campus's student cafe for what was a semi-frequent meet-up for Saturday lunch. Although Seth ate most of his meals on campus at the cafeteria, his meal plan allowed him to periodically transfer a meal to the student cafe.

During the meal, Seth and Dave sat across from one another in a booth. Dave began the get-together by complaining about Seth always ordering the same meal. It was their usual debate, but now Dave had additional ammunition.

"You always get a burger Seth," he said. "Hasn't April loosened you up to trying anything new in life?"

Seth shrugged. "Why mess with what works?"

The campus cafeteria was known for having better meal options than the cafeterias at most other colleges in a multi-state area. However, Seth frequently heard Dave grumble about how those meal options had grown repetitive after living on campus for over three years. In contrast, the cafe had some creative alternatives.

"The food here was better before the renovation," Dave said. "That new catering company that took over the cafeteria just sells the same things here."

The college had installed a remodeled cafe during Seth's sophomore year. In doing so, they had tried to make the cafe cozier, with a range of 'hip' meal options. The menu had jazzy variations of traditional burgers and unusual smoothie combinations.

"Maybe if you hadn't quit," Seth said. "You could have done something about it."

Dave had worked at the cafe as part of a student worker program in order to make extra spending money. It was a relatively easy and conveniently-social job, but it had tightened up after the college outsourced to a food service firm.

"What?" Dave said. "Change it from the inside?"

Seth nodded.

"They fired the head of dining services when he tried that," Dave said.

Unlike most of their lunch meetings, Dave and Seth exchanged little more than their usual food complaints to one another. It was an unusually 'surfacy' conversation.

Seth, feeling pressured to finish his assignments for the semester, had eventually begun reading from a textbook. Finals would begin in under two weeks.

Seth sat back and stretched in his chair, having arrived at a convenient breakpoint in his reading. He looked across his table at Dave, who was working on a series of advanced calculus problems.

"Dave?" Seth asked

Dave continued working, barely acknowledging the question.

"What?" he replied, distracted in thought.

"If I asked you about something," Seth said. "Could you keep it on the down-low?

Dave perked up and sat back from his work.

"Of course," Dave said. "You know me."

"Yeah," Seth said. "I know you."

Seth had second thoughts for a moment, unsure if he should say anything to Dave.

"Look," Dave said. "Who would I tell?"

Seth scoffed. "Right. Anyway, just tell me that you won't go spreading this around. I need your opinion on something."

"I promise," Seth said. "Your secrets are always safe."

"Well," Dave said. "It's about drugs."

Dave's apparent level of excitement continued to rise.

"Finally ready to take up my offer," Dave said. "Eh?"

Seth shook his head. He thought back to the many times that Dave had interrupted his studies in the library with an offer to smoke marijuana behind the library.

"No," Seth said. "That's not it."

"Oh come on," Dave said. "It'll just be the two of us."

"No," Seth said. "It has to do with April."

Dave seemed surprised, but took the remark in stride.

"She needs some weed?" he asked.

"No," Seth said. "It's not that either."

"What is it then? Stop teasing me."

"Have you ever seen April on drugs before?"

Dave thought about the question. "I might've noticed her poking around at some smoke parties."

"Did you ever see her do anything?" Seth asked.

"I don't think so," Dave said. "I never figured she did anything. She seemed too stuck up to have a good time."

Seth groaned at the description of April. "And you guys wonder why I haven't organized that big group hangout with her yet."

"We're fun guys," Dave said. "So it's her loss."

"Anyway," Seth said, "We had a weird run-in with some people at a party last night. A lot of them were doing drugs. She didn't seem bothered by it."

"Some friends of hers?"

"I think so. Old ones."

"If it was the same people who I remember, then, yeah, they liked to party."

A smug look appeared on Dave's face as he guessed Seth's concerns.

"So," Dave said. "What will you do if Miss Jordan wants to smoke up?"

Seth quickly responded. "I don't know."

Dave continued to work the question.

"You're going to judge her like that?" he asked. "Dude, stop sounding so chaste. Aren't you at all curious?"

"Maybe," Seth said, but he quickly backed off. "Not really."

"What if April ends up hiding it? You're wound up about being around people who are just having some fun. If that's the case, she's not going to be open about it."

"That's what I'm worried might be happening."

The tone of Dave's voice switched to a 'big brother' mode.

"Look," he said. "She's probably been doing some stuff, but she knows you'd freak if she said anything."

"I'm not sure," Seth said.

"Would you though?"

"Would I what?"

"Would you freak out?"

Seth immediately said. "No." After a long pause, he admitted. "Maybe."

Dave shook his head over Seth's indecision.

"You need to smoke up with me sometime," Dave said. "It'd take the edge off of things. At the very least, it'll demystify things. You can get past your illogical hang-ups."

"I can't," Seth said.

Dave threw his hands up in the air, clearly frustrated by Seth's teases and subsequent stonewalls.

"Why not?" he asked.

"I have a drug test to take for my med school applications," Seth said. "They aren't big on admitting drug addicts for doctors."

"You're not a drug addict," Dave said. "Try it once and in two weeks, it'll be out of your system. You're perfectly safe."

"What if they take a hair or blood test?" Seth said.

"They won't do that," Dave said.

Seth knew that it was unlikely, but he didn't know for sure. "I'd be dead if they did. Those detect back six months."

"Fine," Dave said. "Keep living in your little world."

The jab made Seth irritable. "I don't need this from you right now. I have enough pressure on me."

"I'm not trying to pressure you," Dave said. "I'm not. But look at how much this girl's already changed you for the better. Do you really want to lose out on that?"

"I know," Seth said, but the tone of his admission wasn't positive. He knew that April had changed him, but he didn't necessarily like some of those changes. "I've been thinking about that."

"You've got this new girlfriend," Dave said. "You're hanging out at Cowboy's. Then you're in the middle of some smoke party."

"It's been quite a month," Seth said.

Seth packed up his bag after deciding that he would be more productive at the library than the cafe.

Before Seth departed, Dave issued a final comment to

him.

"I'm more proud of you now than I've ever been," Dave said. "You're finally living."

Seth did not reply. The sentiment was surely genuine, but Dave could sometimes be painfully theatrical in his observations. He knew that his friends did not understand the uncertainty and discomfort that his relationship with April was causing at times.

20

As the sun set late in the afternoon, its rays cut across the shallow, snow-covered valley that surrounded the college campus. Seth, having completed his studies for the day, was walking with April along a well-maintained sidewalk back to her dorm.

April stopped to admire the sunset.

"I wish that we had the time to do this more often," she said. "The valley looks beautiful tonight."

"Yeah," Seth said, his voice betraying his distracted mind.

Seth had tried to avoid thinking about their relationship throughout the day. Once he was no longer studying, it was hard not to let his mind wander to his recent concerns about April.

"Is everything okay Seth?" April asked. "You haven't seemed happy over the past couple of days."

"I'm fine," Seth said.

"Are you sure?"

Seth let her question linger for a couple of seconds before finally responding. "Can we talk about last weekend?"

"Sure," April said, looking apprehensive. "What is it?"

"When were at that party," Seth said. "You knew all those people coming out of that closet."

Seth looked for some sort of recognition from April, but she did not seem sure where he was going with his statement.

"They're some friends." April said. "I lived near them freshman year, so we've kept in touch."

"Well," Seth said. "I didn't feel comfortable around them."

"Why not?"

Seth tried to figure out a way to be polite but direct in his questioning.

"You didn't think that it was awkward?" he asked.

"No," April said. "They were acting goofy, but some of it was pretty funny."

"Uh-huh," Seth said.

Seth could tell that April was not grasping why he felt confused or upset by her friends. Her explanation only seemed to downplay the prior evening's events.

"They were just some friends unwinding and having fun," she said. "It was not a big deal Seth."

Seth grew annoyed that April didn't seem bothered.

"I'm surprised," he said. "You said yourself that you've seen what drugs can do to people."

April finally seemed to grasp why Seth had been questioning her.

"That's not fair Seth," she said. "Those guys are some of the smartest and hardest-working people I know. It's just to unwind."

"You don't think that it interferes with their lives?" Seth asked.

"If they can handle it," April said. "I don't see a problem."

Seth was silent as the pair continued walking along the sidewalk. Their path, lined with packed snow, ran through a grove of trees.

"Have you ever done anything?" Seth asked.

The question made April appear visibly uncomfortable.

"I didn't until I started dating Bobby," she said. "And it was only once in a while."

The explanation disappointed Seth. He wasn't immediately sure what was causing that thought. It might have been the fact that April had used drugs or it might have been that she had not previously mentioned it.

"Why?" Seth asked.

"I was discovering a lot of new things in my life," April said. "I thought it might bring me closer to him."

Seth's heart sank. He had created a certain image in his mind of April being 'above the fray.' He did not think that she was concerned with what others thought of her. He admired that quality and strength, but it seemed that that image was not entirely correct. "Did it?"

"For a while," April said.

The thought of April being 'closer' with Bobby in either an emotional or physical way only made Seth feel sick.

"Then what happened?" Seth asked.

"Bobby went deeper into some things and couldn't handle it," April said. "He let a lot of things in his life slide."

"So that's why you broke up?" Seth asked.

"Amongst other things." April said.

"But you haven't done anything since?" Seth asked.

At that question, April remained silent for several seconds.

"I knew you'd get upset," she said. "So I didn't say anything."

Seth stammered in surprise. He felt like the conversation was only making things worse rather than better. "What?"

"Last week," April said. "I was with some old friends."

Seth tried to hide his reaction, but he was clearly hurt by her admission. "That disappoints me."

"I'm sorry that I didn't say anything," April said. "I just didn't think that it was a big deal."

Seth shook his head in frustration.

"Even if I was comfortable with you messing around with that stuff," he said. "You haven't been honest with me."

"I'm sorry," April said. "I figured that we'd talk about it, but I wasn't sure when it might be the right time. I wasn't going to keep it a secret."

"I just don't know what to think," Seth said.

The pair continued walking in silence until they reached April's dorm room. They had planned for a quiet evening in her single room, watching a movie together. Seth knew that he would be processing the conversation during the entire movie.

After starting the movie, they settled into April's sofa. Seth glanced at April, their silence lingering. He thought that she looked remorseful, but she was not entirely repentant.
They had just shared their first fight as a couple. Seth didn't feel like spending the evening arguing over the same point again. At the same time, he knew that he would have a hard time forgetting about it.

21

The next day – Sunday afternoon – Seth met up with his friends to play a game of intramural soccer. Despite being crushed with school work and his relationship with April, he still took time to be on the team. If anything, it was a forced workout obligation when he would not have otherwise made the time.

The games were held at a large, indoor field that was part of a college recreation complex. Players on both Seth's team and the opposing team sported brightly-colored team jerseys. There was not much in the way of a crowd, although April was there to cheer along Seth's team.

Before the game was underway, players on both teams sprinted around on the field. The ball moved in fast flashes when kicked on the semi-smooth artificial turf playing surface.

The teams soon broke from their warm-ups and headed to huddles on opposite ends of the field. Seth, Dave, Tony, and Mark all huddled together, along with several other students who were on their team.

Mark, their captain, gave a quick pep-talk.

"This is just for fun," Mark said. "But we're not losing to some old guys."

Mark glanced over at the other team's huddle. The guys on that team looked to be mostly older, in their thirties. Seth knew that they were a mix of Park College alumni and other members of the Winneshiek community.

"Stay sharp and follow our game plan," Mark continued.

The huddle broke as the players took their positions for the initial kick-off.

Seth's mind was on the game, but he still heard April cheering.

"Go Seth!" she yelled.

Seth smiled at April. He did not usually like attention at the games, but he did not usually have a beautiful girl on the sidelines giving him that attention. Part of Seth was still mesmerized by the sheer idea that he was dating April, despite the discomfort between them during the past few days.

Mark took the kick-off and passed the ball over to Seth. Striking the ball ahead, Seth dodged a number of the other team's defenders. In fact, he made it all the way down the field with surprising ease. At least until a leg crossed in front of him, knocking him onto his stomach.

At first, Seth had no idea what had occurred. He felt as though he had almost blacked out from the fall, unsure if he had been tripped or was somehow caught up with a defender. As he stood up, a helping hand extended down to him. When Seth looked up, he found that the hand belonged to Bobby.

Seth had not noticed Bobby during the warm-up period prior to the game. As a result, he was shocked that Bobby had turned up on the opposing team.

"Always be on the lookout kid!" Bobby said, giving Seth a condescending smirk.

In the meantime, Mark had recovered the ball and kicked it back in Dave's direction. Bobby ran to defend Dave while Seth moved into a parallel position.

The ball was passed from Dave back to Seth, who tried to remember some of the plays that Mark had given them.

From their team's goal at the opposite end of the field, Seth heard Tony yell out. "Knock it in there!"

Seth increased his speed with the ball, sailing past two defenders. He was again putting on a one-man show, sprinting down the field as quickly as he had a minute prior. This time, Seth noticed Bobby approaching, acting as his team's final defender until the goal.

Bobby tried to sneak another cheap shot at Seth, but Seth sensed it coming. He made Bobby look foolish by doing a quick double-back with the ball. Bobby lost his footing on the turf and slid onto his back.

Seth ran at an angle, his path clear to the goal and his eyes on the goalie. When the timing was right, Seth swung his leg back and nailed the ball past the helpless goalie.

Dave and Mark both ran over to give Seth high-fives. Seth felt vindicated as he glanced over his shoulder at Bobby. Bobby was back on his feet, but looking at Seth with the same smirk as before. Seth knew that it would be a long game.

As the players moved into position for the next kick-off, Seth looked to his team's sideline for April. She was standing attentive, politely observing, but no longer actively cheering.

22

Seth's team went on to win the afternoon's soccer game, but he had little time for celebration. After dinner, Seth headed over to the library. He planned to be there for the duration of the evening.

Not wanting to be disturbed, Seth did not go to his usual lower-level study spot. Instead, he had found a large, square table in the library's upper floor. After several hours, he had books piled around the table. He flipped through them while scribbling on a notepad.

The seeming peace ended when a large book flew from behind Seth, sailing over his shoulder. It landed on the tabletop and slid across it before falling to the floor. Seth looked up to see Tony peering at him from behind a bookshelf.

"You need something?" Seth asked.

"I figured that you had time for a study break." Tony said.

"Well..." Seth began, ready with an excuse. His words cut off after he noticed that Tony had a guest with him. Tony led a girl by the hand over to Seth's library table. The pair took a seat on the tabletop.

Seth tried without success to place the girl before giving Tony a confused look.

"I wanted to introduce you to someone," Tony said.

The girl gave Seth a dumb wave and a smile.

"This is my girlfriend," Tony said. "Rosey."

Seth was surprised at the announcement. It was rare for Tony to introduce one of the girls in his life as a 'girlfriend.'

"My friends call me Skippy." Rosey said.

"Uh-huh," Tony said. He shrugged his shoulders at Seth

as if to say "Whatever."

"Have you known each other for very long?" Seth asked.

"No," Rosey said. "We just met last week."

"Really?" Seth asked.

"Yep," Rosey said. "Tony was such a gentleman."

"Remember that night when we were at Cowboy's?" Tony asked Seth.

Seth thought back to that evening. After putting things together, he replied with a dry tone. "Oh, of course."

Tony's demeanor was oddly corny and cutesy toward Rosey.

"I swept you off your feet," he said. "Didn't I?"

"Yes he did," Rosey said. "Most guys act like that bar is a meat market."

"Not Tony?" Seth asked.

"Nope," Rosey said. "Not Tony. He was so nice to me."

Tony seemed to make almost-nervous conversation with Seth. "Where'd you ever disappear to that night?"

"I went home and crashed," Seth said. "With your car. Remember?"

Tony had to think about things for a moment. He did not appear to remember Seth taking his car back to campus for him.

"Oh yeah," he said. "Did all of the excitement that night sap the party animal out of you? Or was it something else?"

Seth gave Tony a dirty look.

Tony ignored the glare and said to Rosey. "Seth had to run home to his little girlfriend."

"Oh Tony," Rosey said. "Be nice."

Rosey had a sympathetic tone to her voice when she asked Seth. "Who's that?"

"You mind if I tell her?" Tony asked.

Seth found the request odd, but thus far, much of the conversation had been odd. He assumed that it would not matter.

"Why not?" Seth said. "I'm sure that you will anyway."

Tony whispered into Rosey's ear. Her eyes became wide.

"April Jordan!" Rosey said. "She's your girlfriend?"

"Yes," Seth said.

"Really?" Rosey asked.

Seth was both annoyed and amused by Rosey's apparent disbelief. "Really."

"For how long?"

"About five weeks," Seth said.

Rosey's face twisted, as though she could not process the information. "That doesn't make any sense!"

"Jeeez," Tony said. "Keep it down honey. We're in a library."

"Sorry baby," Rosey said. "I just can't believe it's her. I live next door to her, so I know all about her."

At that point, Seth could feel the hair on his arms tingling. He felt the same dread that he had felt during his visit to Cowboy's and to the house party the prior week. He knew that something awful was likely coming.

"You know all about her." Seth repeated Rosey's assertion. His voice was flat. "Really?"

"Really," Rosey said. She was obviously surprised. "How well do you know her?"

"Pretty well," Seth said. "We've been dating."

Rosey appeared skeptical. "How come I've never seen you around?"

Seth gave her the question right back. "How come I've never seen you?"

"Hmm," Rosey said. "The only guy I ever see her with is Bobby. They kept me up all last night."

The statement made Seth feel as though he had been hit by a hammer. He stammered. "What're you talking about?"

Tony tried to cut Rosey off before she could continue with any details.

"I'm sorry," Tony said to Seth. "I'm sure Rosey is mixed up."

Seth's mind was reeling. After his uncomfortable movie viewing with April the prior night, he had gone back to his dorm room alone. Even though Seth could not accept that April would be the kind of person to cheat on him, the timing and circumstances seemed horribly plausible.

No," Seth said. "I'd like to hear what she has to say."

"If you're together," Rosey said, warning him. "I don't think you'll like it."

Seth rubbed his face. Part of him wanted to forget about it, but the other part of him knew that he had to hear her story.

"Tell me," Seth said.

Rosey took a deep breath.

"I couldn't sleep at all last night," she said. "It would be quiet for a few seconds and then this banging would start again."

Seth had a vivid imagination that worked overtime as Rosey told her story. He imagined moonlight creeping through a dorm window, illuminating Rosey's bed as she lay tossing and turning.

A banging noise emanated from the center of the wall next to the bed. It stopped long enough for Rosey to close her eyes, but then started again a few seconds later.

"Then she was laughing," Rosey said. "I mean it was just SO loud."

The banging noise disappeared underneath April's sudden, hysterical laugh. She was loud enough to send a shiver down any listener's spine.

"Then," Rosey said. "He was yelling out stuff about her. It was like they were in my room."

Seth knew that the dorm room walls seemed to be paper thin at times. He imagined how Bobby could be heard talking from inside Rosey's room.

"Baby," Rosey had heard Bobby saying. "You're like an animal tonight. What's gotten into you?"

Seth could not shake the images out of his mind.

"Then the weird stuff happened," Rosey said. "It sounded like the zoo had moved in next door."

Seth pictured Rosey shaking her head in amazement and disgust. The noises only grew louder. April was heard making short dog noises. Bobby joined in.

"So I was wondering what to do," Rosey said. "I didn't need to be up all night."

Rosey banged her fists against the wall. Her effort did little to quiet the noise.

The sounds coming from the other side of the wall became a jumble of overlapping noises. There was a general pounding noise mixed with intermittent laughing, groaning, and barking.

"I'd heard those two getting weird in the past," Rosey said. "But last night was crazy. It was incredible."

Seth could not say a word in response. He sat slumped in his chair, feeling as though he needed to cry.

Rosey continued talking, animated as ever. "I thought that

it was over between those two. I guess that it wasn't."

Seth noticed Tony rubbing his hands together. He was annoyed that Tony didn't seem at all sympathetic to what had been a devastating story.

"If I were you, I'd get away from that girl." Rosey said. "She's weird. Weird, like some kind of freak show."

23

Seth was so angry after hearing Rosey's story that he gathered up his books and left the library. On his way outside, he asked Tony to speak with him in private. They walked out into the cold night together and headed for Seth's dorm room.

Seth felt adrift. He was no longer sure what to think or believe. As soon as Rosey had bid Tony goodbye, Seth grilled him.

"Is it true?" Seth asked.

Tony played dumb. "Is what true?"

"All that stuff that she said," Seth said. He assumed that Tony had spent the prior night with Rosey and could easily confirm the validity of the story.

"What stuff?" Tony asked.

Seth grew frustrated. "Don't play stupid. That stuff that your girlfriend said about April."

"I was sleeping," Tony said. "But, yeah, it's probably true. Rosey isn't a girl who makes stuff like that up."

"You didn't get woken up by anything?"

"You know how I am after I've been drinking," Tony said. "A neutron bomb wouldn't have woken me up."

"Dammit," Seth said, disgusted.

"Listen," Tony said. "All that story does is tell you that she's a little freaky. You don't want to let that scare you off of her."

Seth looked down at the sidewalk in front of him.

"She cheated on me," he said.

For once, Tony was speechless.

"Things were going so well too," Seth said. "At least, I thought they were, until the past few days."

Seth kicked at a pile of snow along the sidewalk. He felt embarrassed. He was also mad at himself for having wasted so much of his time on April.

"No man," Tony said. "This changes everything."

"Yeah," Seth said. "It means that it's over. I've been played like a fool for five weeks."

Tony tried to get Seth to calm down.

"No," Tony said. "Jeez, no. This is an opportunity."

Seth was surprised by Tony's suggestion. "You just watched me get humiliated and that's your advice?"

"Think about it," Tony said. "Now you've got a free pass. She made her mistake. Now you have some leverage if you happened to have an opportunity with another girl. Trust me, it can be handy to have."

"I don't want a free pass," Seth said. "I don't want to date anyone else."

"Mark said that you guys had a fight last night," Tony said.

"Yeah," Seth said.

"It was probably just a one-time thing with this Bobby," Tony said. "No offense, but she's a little freaky and needs it. Don't blow this when you could use it to your advantage."

Seth again tried to ignore the suggestion, but Tony continued making his sales pitch.

"The old boyfriend had probably been lurking around just in case you guys didn't work out," Tony said. "Patch it up with April, but be firm. Let her know who's boss and put her in her place."

"I can't believe that you think that April cheating on me is supposed to encourage me."

"Stuff happens," Tony said. "Like I said, be firm. Rock her world a little bit."

By this point in the conversation, Seth was thoroughly distracted by his angry thoughts.

"Oh," he said. "I'll rock her world."

24

Rather than immediately confronting the situation, Seth let his thoughts stew. His mind further twisted in on itself. He ignored April over the remainder of the weekend and throughout the next day. Such avoidance was a task not easily done, given the small size of Park College and its insular nature,

The next evening, Seth sat at his desk, scribbling on a notebook. He had been distracted through most of his classes that day and had accomplished nothing that evening. Realizing that he would only further waste time by delaying what seemed inevitable, he picked up his phone and dialed April's number.

She answered. "Hi."

"Hi," Seth said.

April's speech was a whisper, barely heard through the receiver.

"There's a voice that I haven't heard from in a while," April said. "Where have you been the past couple of days? Mark said that you were busy and I was worried."

"Sorry that we haven't talked much. I've had a lot going on," Seth said. "Studying. Projects. I guess that I got distracted by some things."

"I have two tests tomorrow," April said. Seth could tell from the tone in her voice that she had been crying. "It's probably best that we've had some time apart."

Seth suspected that her cheerful spin was a lie. He knew about her two tests, but she had never previously made comments about how being apart was necessarily a positive thing.

After letting the silence linger, April finally asked what was an obvious question. "Is something wrong Seth?"

Seth knew that they needed to talk, but he had been dreading the pain that was sure to be involved. "You need a study break?"

"Sure," April said.

"How about some racquetball?" Seth asked, regretting the suggestion as soon as it had come out of his mouth. It would only waste time before they discussed things.

"Sounds great," April said, her tone not at all excited.

"I'll come right over," Seth said.

"I'll be waiting," April said.

Seth took quick strides down the long entry-hallway to April's dorm. There was a stairwell at the end of the hallway with paths that led either down or up.

While still a distance from the stairwell, Seth halted at the sight of Bobby descending the stairs. Bobby stopped. Both men stared at one another, each almost indifferent to the other.

Bobby then continued walking around the stairwell, descending into the dorm's lower depths.

An instant later, Seth approached the stairwell, jogging up the stairs to April's room.

The racquetball match had been as awkward as Seth had feared. Neither he nor April was adept at confrontation. They spent thirty minutes playing a game of racquetball in which Seth knew neither had any interest.

After finishing the game, Seth and April emerged together from the recreation center. Seth was still sweaty under his clothes, a fact that made the cold seem even chillier than normal.

April glanced over at Seth and smiled, trying to break the tension between them.

"It looks like there's smoke coming off your head," April said.

"Must be the cold," Seth said. His voice was flat.

The pair strode together along a lighted path that led to the dorms. Seth kept trying to figure out how to bring up what he had learned. Finally, April beat him to it.

"I was hoping that we'd get a chance to talk more about

what you said the other day," April said. "I have some things to add."

"There's some things that I'd like to say too."

Seth studied April's reaction, but he couldn't tell if she looked relieved or worried.

"Good," April said. "I don't think you should be upset about what I did with my friends."

"There might have been a time when I'd have agreed with you," Seth said. "It's more than that now."

"Why? April asked, confused. "What does that mean?"

"I'd like to talk about Bobby," Seth said. "Your old boyfriend."

April continued to have a confused expression on her face.

"I don't understand," she said. "I already told you about him. We haven't been together for months."

"That's interesting," Seth said. "I ran into him tonight on the way to your room."

April paused as if trying to consider where Seth was going with the conversation.

"He stopped over this evening," April said. "But I told him that I didn't have time to visit. I've tried to be friends with him, but maybe that isn't a good idea if it's going to cause problems with us."

"Is that all it was?" Seth asked.

"Of course," April said.

Seth tried reading April, looking for any sign that might tell him that she was not making up excuses.

"If he'd been bothering you," Seth said. "Why didn't you ask for help?"

"I didn't need any help," April said. "He wasn't bothering me."

"What was he doing then?"

"He was passing by and stopped in for a visit. I made him leave so that I could go out with you."

"Really?"

The tone of April's voice changed. It turned softer.

"Calm down Seth," she said. "You don't need to get angry."

Seth could feel the blood rushing to his face.

"I'm not angry," he said. "I'm upset about being left out of the loop."

"What's that supposed to mean?" April asked. "I thought that you wanted to talk about what happened at the party. Why are we talking about Bobby?"

Seth finally said it. "I know that you're still sleeping with him."

April looked shocked by the accusation. "What?"

Having finally laid out the accusation, Seth was not sure whether he was about to explode in rage or collapse from the pain of his broken heart. "Why don't you just tell me the truth?"

"The truth?" April asked.

"Everyone else on campus seems to know what's going on," Seth said. "I just want you to tell me. I want you to say it to my face."

"For you to stand here and say these things..." April said. She stopped talking as tears streamed down her cheeks.

"Say what?" Seth asked. "That you were sneaking around behind my back?"

"Stop saying that."

"Did he give you a free hit once in a while too? Was that it?"

April pleaded with Seth to calm down. "Why're you behaving like this?"

"It wasn't very hard to put two and two together April," Seth said.

"I have no idea what you're talking about," April said. "It sounds like you're either paranoid or confused."

For a moment, Seth wondered if he had somehow been wrong. Had he misjudged the evidence that had piled up over the past several days? Ultimately, Seth knew that he had to trust his analysis and instincts.

"I'm not the one who's apparently confused," Seth said.

April began walking away from Seth. After several steps, she stopped and turned around to face him. Tears continued flowing down her cheeks.

"I thought that maybe you were different," April said. "I guess that I was wrong."

"You're not the only one who was wrong," Seth said.

25

Later that evening, Seth stretched out on the sofa in his room for what seemed to him like hours. He had kept the room pitch black inside, preferring to shut out any distractions while he tried to process how his world had so radically changed during the past several days.

Seth was startled when he heard a key go into his room's deadbolt lock.

The room door swung open and Mark stepped inside, flipping on a light. Seth ignored him, moving from the sofa to his desk chair. He wanted his back to Mark, so that Mark couldn't see that he had been crying.

"Everything all right?" Mark asked.

Seth had not planned on having to rehash everything with Mark that evening. He had assumed that Mark would be with Melissa and that he would have the room to himself.

"I don't want to talk about it," Seth said.

Mark was taken aback by the curt reply.

"Hey buddy," he said. "I come in and I see my roommate looking down, sitting alone in the dark. It would appear that something is wrong."

Seth kept staring out the window, continuing to keep his back to Mark.

"It's over," he said.

Mark didn't seem to understand what Seth meant. "What's over?"

"April." Seth said. "I broke it off tonight."

"Why? I thought you said that things were going well?"

"They were. Sort of. I found out yesterday that she was..."

Seth stopped talking. It was too hard for him to get it all out. He felt humiliated and, deep down, inadequate. He knew that he'd have to explain things to people and that thought weighed heavily on him. His confidence had been shattered.

Seth finally blurted out the rest of the explanation. "She was still with that guy."

Mark looked surprised by the revelation.

"Are you sure?" he asked. "I thought that she said that was over a long time ago?"

"No," Seth said. "It wasn't. I saw him leaving her dorm tonight. Tony's new girlfriend had some stories too."

Mark was quiet in thought for a few moments. When he finally spoke, his response was not what Seth had anticipated.

"Tony has a girlfriend?" Mark asked.

"Yeah," Seth said, annoyed. "It's a long story. Anyway, I just feel like part of it was my fault."

Mark was confused. "How could this be your fault?"

Seth finally glanced back at Mark. By this point, his eyes were bloodshot and his face was flushed from emotion.

"I must not have stacked up," Seth said, admitting his gravest concern about the situation. "Maybe she got tired of me and wanted to go back to him. Like I was the greener grass, but then I wasn't anymore."

So far as Seth knew, Mark had never encountered a similar situation. Mark was not the sort of person to whom such things happened. A girl would not cheat on him.

"I doubt that's the case man," Mark said. "She was the one dating up here. You're one of the smartest guys on campus. You've got a bright future. Rich, powerful."

"I don't know that those were her top criteria."

"I never told you something Seth," Mark said. "But now is a decent time to share it."

Seth wasn't sure where Mark was headed. "What is it?"

"Remember that girl who I was dating before Melissa?" Mark said. "Jenny."

"Maybe," Seth said. He'd only just begun getting to know Mark during that time in his life, but Seth had the vague memory of a girl whom Mark had seen immediately prior to Melissa.

"Just don't be telling all this to the guys," Mark said. "Jenny and I had been dating for a few weeks. Then one day, bam, she's not returning my phone calls."

"Really?" Seth asked.

"Yeah, like I said, this kind of thing never happened to me. I lost it for a little and tried to figure out what was going on. When I finally talked to her, she gave me some nonsense answers about not being interested anymore. The next thing I knew, I saw her around campus with some guy who she used to date."

"She'd still been with him?"

"I don't know," Mark said. "I could have gone crazy second guessing things like that. All you can do is pick yourself up and move on."

The suggestion rang hollow to Seth.

"It's not that easy," he said.

"I know it's not," Mark said. "Do you think it was for a guy like me? Even after I started dating Melissa, it screwed things up for a while with her. I didn't trust women for a long time after that."

Seth was silent for a moment. He knew that Mark ultimately had a point. He could not completely shut down, even if that was what he was aching to do.

"I'll try," Seth said.

26

With final exams for the first semester looming, Seth tried to return to his routine over the next several days. His routine was his usual method of coping with the different challenges that he faced. Moving on from April felt to him like one of his most significant challenges yet.

Park College's final exam system allowed for a number of 'study days' prior to the actual testing. Seth spent most of his waking hours during that time at the library.

Seth's friends, particularly Mark and Dave, tried to break some of the tension that they knew Seth was going through during those days. As was typical though, their efforts tended to be rather counterproductive.

In one instance, Seth left his study desk in order to check out a practice exam from the reference department. When he returned to his desk, all of his books were missing. Mark and Dave, who were sitting nearby, both had guilty looks on their faces.

"Where'd you put my stuff?" Seth asked, annoyed. He'd been through this game with them in the past.

Both Mark and Dave mimed to Seth, indicating that they did not know what could have occurred.

As Seth surveyed the area around his study desk, Mark and Dave quietly stood up from their desks. Seth noticed Mark grab a hidden book bag from a nearby low shelf.

Soon, Seth was running past several library patrons in close pursuit of Mark and Dave. While they ran, the two tossed Seth's backpack back and forth over bookshelves like a football.

Eventually, Seth stopped Dave with a solid tackle on the

library carpet.

As Seth looked up in victory, he saw Professor Lee standing in a nearby aisle, shaking his head.

During the study days, it was not unusual for Seth to end up spending late evenings at the campus computer lab. Not every class had a final exam, but some instead required final papers to be written. In other cases, Seth needed a computer with specialized software.

Illustrating how exhausted he'd become, Seth woke up one night to a computer screen full of the letter 'Z.' He had been working into the middle of the night on reworking advanced calculus assignments and he had fallen asleep on a corner of the computer's keyboard.

Part of the Seth's return to routine involved rejoining his friends for their usual dining gatherings. The people watching seemed as trite as usual to Seth, but it provided a distraction for him.

That attempt to be distracted was not a complete success. Seth was often still reminded of April when he caught glimpses of her during lunch or dinner. He would wonder how he'd never noticed her until that past autumn. It was one of the ironies of life that people, sometimes even the beautiful people, often went unnoticed until they suddenly mattered.

During one particular lunch, Seth observed April walking in his direction. He immediately grew tense, thinking that she might be coming near, potentially even planning to sit at his table.

Ultimately, neither Seth nor April explicitly acknowledged one another. April's path changed as she sat down at an empty table near where Seth was seated with his friends. Her back was turned to him. She sat alone.

Despite the distractions, Seth completed his final exams feeling as though he had performed reasonably well on them. At the very least, he was certain that they had not turned into the disaster that he had initially feared they might become.

After finals concluded, Seth had one last evening on campus before heading home the next morning for winter break. Many students had already left for home that evening, but many of those who stuck around found their way to parties at homes off-campus.

Mark had invited Seth along to one such party, being held by the school's happy-go-lucky rugby club. True to the club's reputation, Seth was not surprised that the event was a crowded, wild house party. It was already in full swing by the time he and Mark arrived.

Groups of students streamed through the front door as stacks of plastic cups were distributed. Seth didn't spend much time socializing. He knew few people in the club and knew even fewer of their associated friends.

Amid the laughing and yelling, Seth quietly sat his cup down and headed for the door. Before he could leave, Seth felt a hand on his shoulder. Turning around, he discovered Mark giving him a disappointed look.

"Just where are you going?" Mark asked.

"I can't stay any longer," Seth said. "I need to get packed up. I wanted to leave early tomorrow morning."

"You've always got some excuse man," Mark said, smiling and shaking his head.

The house party that Seth had attended was only a few blocks from campus. It was a chilly mid-December evening outside, but, after being at the uncomfortably warm house party, Seth found the walk back to campus to be refreshing.

Seth's route took him within a short block of Cowboy's Bar, its neon sign in the distance. He walked past the bar, paying little attention until he heard hurried footsteps approaching him. The sound heralded a bundled-up figure running toward Seth. As the figure raced past him, their shoulder brushed Seth's arm.

Seth looked closely and realized that, beneath the layers of winter clothing, the passerby had been Rosey. She stopped in front of Cowboy's and headed inside. Before she disappeared, Seth observed that her face appeared puffy or swollen.

Seth waited near the exterior of Cowboy's for a moment,

considering the unusual sight. He was standing out of direct view when the front door to Cowboy's swung open. Rosey reappeared with a drunken Tony in tow.

Tony was laughing, bent over and clearly drunk. Rosey proceeded to hit and kick him.

"You're the slimeball everyone said you were," Rosey said.

Tony tried in vain to protect himself.

"Baby," he said. "She's just a friend."

Rosey kicked Tony again. This time, it seemed to register. He bent over in pain and didn't stand back up.

"That's what you said last time," Rosey said. "You had your hands all over that freshman whore."

"Baby," Tony said. "You know you're the only girl for me. You're my Venus."

"I'm better than your act."

Rosey walked off into the darkness, leaving Tony behind as he fell to the ground. He was a mess, coughing and trying to catch his breath.

Seth waited for Rosey to disappear and came to Tony's aide. Tony was surprised to see Seth, but did not coherently respond for several seconds.

"You okay?" Seth asked, helping Tony to his feet.

"I'm fine man," Tony said, still disoriented from a combination of alcohol and pain. "Hey, can we go back inside? I want you to meet someone."

27

Winter Break lasted for nearly three weeks. Seth visited with family and spent an evening catching up with friends from high school. During much of that time, Seth had his focus on the medical school entrance exam – the MCAT. He also had April still looming in his head. Thoughts of her easily rose to the surface without the pressure of looming finals to distract him.

The time flew by quickly. Soon enough, Seth's final semester at Park College was set to begin.

When Seth returned to campus, he still had the MCAT firmly on his mind. He spent the evening before classes were to resume studying for it in his usual spot in the library.

Not long after he had begun reviewing notes, Seth noticed Mark emerge from an isle directly behind him. Seth pretended not to notice as Mark removed a book from the shelf and threw it in his direction.

At the last moment, Seth moved out of the book's flight path. It missed Seth's shoulder, instead slamming against the back of his study desk. Seth turned around to face his assailant.

"Jerk," Seth said.

"You'd have taken the shot too," Mark said. "If you'd had it."

Seth laid down a pen to mark a spot in his book.

"Only out of retaliation for all the times that you'd done it to me" Seth said. "What's going on? I'm in the middle of stuff."

"You're always in the middle of something," Mark said. "Melissa and I wanted to invite you down to Philly's for dinner after the library closed."

Seth knew that the library would close by early-evening, as

it was still operating under limited 'break' hours. The invitation also reminded him that the cafeteria would not be open that evening either. His only option was eating out.

"That sounds fine," he said.

"Good," Mark said. "Melissa will be at Philly's early, but I'll catch up with you guys after I run some errands. Keep her company for me, okay?"

Seth hesitated, not wanting to stretch out the evening. He didn't want to be rude though and could spare the time.

"Okay," he said.

Mark winked and added. "You know that you're the only friend of mine who she likes, right?"

When Seth entered the Philadelphia Bar and Grill, he found the restaurant empty, the bar modestly populated with locals. As expected, Mark had not yet arrived, but Melissa was seated alone at a booth to the rear. Seth headed in her direction.

"Mind if I join you?" Seth asked.

"Only if you buy me a drink," Melissa said.

"Maybe."

Melissa winked at Seth. "You won't get lucky if you don't."

The banter was playful, but not entirely flirty. Seth held up his hand for attention. A moment later, a waiter stepped over to the table

"I need a drink for the lady," Seth said.

Melissa looked up at the waiter.

"Sex on the beach," she said.

"Kinky," Seth said.

"Always," Melissa said. She took a long look at Seth. He couldn't help but feel like she was sizing him up.

Even though Melissa was Mark's girlfriend, Seth hadn't had much time to speak with her during the past several weeks. Given the hectic time around final exams that followed and the natural distance of the winter break, they had barely discussed his break up with April.

Seth and Melissa next finished their food order. After the waiter had departed from their booth, they settled into conversation.

"What's new with you Seth?" Melissa asked.

"Not much," Seth said. "The MCAT is in a couple of weeks. I'll have an anatomy lab starting right away tomorrow."

"But you're actually taking an evening off tonight?"

"Maybe. I probably won't have many nights off after class starts again."

Melissa's eyes made her appear as though she was strategizing.

"Seth," she said. "Promise me that you'll enjoy the next few months."

"I will," Seth said. "At least after I take the MCAT and have some med school applications sent off."

A devilish gleam continued to appear in Melissa's eyes.

"Maybe you'll find somebody," she said.

Seth wasn't surprised that it had not taken her long to center the conversation on his love life. Unfortunately, he wasn't particularly interested in discussing it. Over the winter break, he had made up his mind that he would not be pursuing any new relationships.

"Why would I do that?" he asked. "The year's almost over. I don't need another distraction. Not again."

"The timing is perfect though," Melissa said.

"Why's that?"

"No commitments. Have some fun with somebody. Try some things out."

Seth thought about it for a moment, but a flood of excuses came to mind.

"I can't do that," he said.

"Why not?" Melissa asked. "What have you got to lose?"

"I'm not that kind of a guy."

Melissa scoffed. "You still don't know what sort of a guy you are, nor do you need to know. Have fun."

"I'll have fun," Seth said. "Just in my own way, that's all."

The waiter arrived with Melissa's drink. She sipped at it.

"Besides that whole April Jordan thing," Melissa said. "You've had, like, one other girlfriend in four years."

The comment made Seth withdraw. As proud as he was of his academic achievements, he was not proud of his dating record.

"So," Seth said.

"And why has that been?" Melissa asked.

"You tell me," Seth said. "I'm sure that you have some ideas."

"I think there's an explanation somewhere in that big head."

Seth didn't like the tone of Melissa's remark. She was being unusually pushy and he became defensive.

"Like I said," he said. "Why don't you save me the trouble and do the explaining?"

"Maybe you could remind me why things ended with that one girl" Melissa said. "What was her name?"

"Sheila."

"Sheila," Melissa said. "Whatever happened there?"

Seth continued to 'massage' the truth behind his relationship with Sheila. In this telling though, he was marginally more accurate with the details.

"One day," he said. "We both realized that we'd changed too much during college. She'd been dating a guy in the past. It was long distance with us, so I got jealous when he still seemed to be lurking around. She made some bad choices."

In Seth's mind, this was true. He might have been dumped by Sheila, but he'd also hesitated with her. He had been intimidated by her past dating history.

"Hang on," Melissa said. "This was Sheila having an old boyfriend who made you jealous? Or April?"

"Sheila," Seth said. "Both I guess."

"Did she actually cheat on you too?" Melissa asked. "Or she wasn't perfect enough for Seth?"

"I was intimidated at the time," Seth said. "That might have been some of it, but I don't know for sure. I thought that I did at the time though. She liked to party too and was comfortable in that scene. I wasn't."

Melissa took another sip of her drink and scolded Seth.

"No one's perfect Seth," she said.

"I know that," Seth said. He did not sound entirely convincing.

"What's happened since Sheila?"

"You know that I've been focused on school. Every time I met someone who was interesting, something usually came up right away that made dating a non-starter."

Seth shrugged. This had turned into his 'usual'

conversation with Melissa, but she was being more aggressive than in the past.

"They don't measure up," Melissa said. "So you don't pursue things?"

"I don't know about that," Seth said. "I know that it sounds like I was being rash sometimes, but I'd find out stuff about the girl from the guys."

"They're good at that."

Seth knew that they were. The problem with his friends was that they always seemed to find a flaw in every single girl on campus. Having a 'background check' available was often a dual-edged sword.

"Well," Seth said. "I didn't want to be with some girl who had been sleeping around with half the guys on campus. Or someone who was always hanging out at the bars. That's just not who I am. It wouldn't have worked."

"What about April?" Melissa asked.

"What about her?"

"Were there things in her past that bothered you?"

Seth scoffed.

"Well yeah," he said. "She cheated on me."

"I'm not asking about that," Melissa said. "I meant before that."

Seth knew what Melissa was trying to learn if he had issues with April prior to her cheating.

"Not necessarily," Seth said, hesitating. "I don't know."

"What was it then?" Melissa said. "What was bothering you?"

The question was interrupted when the waiter returned with their food. During the brief pauses in conversation, Seth decided that he might as well open up about it. He'd kept things bottled up long enough.

"There were a few things," he said. "Before the cheating stuff came up. I'd never been to Cowboy's before, but I went there with the guys one night. It turned out that she used to hang out there quite a bit. It seemed too foreign to me."

"You were mad that she went to a bar?"

"No, but I hadn't imagined her liking a place like that. I had a particular idea about who she was. That didn't fit into it."

Melissa seemed to understand. "Okay."

"Then," Seth said. "The next day, we were at a party where I found out about some drug stuff. That bugged me."

"She had a drug problem?" Melissa asked.

"I don't think so," Seth said. "It was just another surprise to me. A big surprise. It was something that I couldn't reconcile about her."

Seth picked at his food, trying to figure out how to explain what had happened next.

"Things kept popping in my head after that," he continued. "Things with her and her friends. Things that maybe I imagined were likely a part of her past."

Melissa gave Seth a disappointed look.

"Assumptions then," she said. "You assumed that she had behaved in a way that might have offended you or made you uncomfortable."

Seth thought about Melissa's assertion for a moment. "Probably."

"Let's say that some of that stuff that you were speculating about had actually happened," Melissa said. "Even if she regretted some of those things, what could she do about the past?"

"Not much," Seth said. "I know that you're right, but that still didn't make it easy."

Melissa smiled at Seth. "I didn't mean to say that it would make it easy."

Seth was surprised by how much better it made him feel to get some of his hang-ups off of his chest.

"There was one other thing," he said. "Even before the cheating or the drug stuff came up, I was confused over why she had stayed with Bobby for so long. The idea of them together in the first place, I could never figure it out."

"Did that intimidate you too?" Melissa asked. "Knowing that she'd been in a long-term relationship while you hadn't?"

"A little bit," Seth said. "I kept waiting for the other shoe to drop. I figured that she'd realize that I was this guy who didn't know what he was doing."

Seth felt pathetic. For as much confidence as he usually had in himself, he realized how little confidence he had in his dating skills.

"Now you think that's what happened?" Melissa asked. "That's why she cheated on you?"

"Maybe," Seth said. "It made it all so much worse when I found out that I'd been right all along."

"You don't know if that was entirely the case," Melissa said. "Even if you did, you can't live life expecting the worst out of people."

Seth knew that she was right, but the excuses helped to comfort him.

"We were similar in some ways," Seth said. "But also very different."

"There's nothing wrong with that," Melissa said. "I've found that some differences can be a good thing. If you can grow together."

Normally that advice would have seemed encouraging to Seth, but he was not sure how apt it was to his situation with April.

"Well," he said. "I didn't see myself growing into being a party guy."

"Maybe that's not what she wanted." Melissa said. "When you found yourself with someone like her in the future, it sounds like you should talk more openly about your concerns. Especially if you're running with your imagination instead of asking questions."

"Yeah, I wish I'd thought about that at the time. Instead, she probably thought that I'd suddenly turned into a moody weirdo."

"Don't beat yourself up. Just remember it for next time."

Seth tried not to dwell on his misstep, but he knew that it would be hard.

"Why do interesting people always have something about them that ends up turning me off?" Seth asked.

"The most interesting people usually have the most complicated pasts," Melissa said, smirking. "That's a part of what makes them interesting."

Seth thought about the point and smiled. "Maybe I need to find someone who's only half-interesting. Balance it out."

Melissa shook her head. "It won't ever work that way. The easiest thing is for you to accept people for who they are now and not expect perfection."

Seth reflected back on how messy things had become with April. He'd gone over different aspects of his relationship with

April in his head for what seemed like a million times. However, he'd never verbalized all of it to anyone. Everything had been a jumbled mess in his head.

"I've grown a lot over these four years in college," Seth said. "Maybe next time I'll figure the girl out before it goes wrong."

"I hope so," Melissa said. "I'm not saying that it was your fault that she cheated. There's no excuse for that. I just think that maybe you had some problems that could have been addressed without souring the relationship."

"That's an understatement."

Seth was grateful for the unexpected conversation. For what seemed like the first time in weeks, he felt like he could relax his mind regarding April.

"If you ever find yourself in a similar situation," Melissa said. "I'm sure that you'll handle it differently."

Mark arrived as the conversation was winding down. He made his way over to Seth and Melissa's table, oblivious to the discussion that had just occurred.

"What've you girls been up to?" Mark asked.

Melissa gave Mark a mock-disgusted look.

"This is what I deal with Seth," Melissa said. "He's not perfect."

Melissa removed Mark's arm from her shoulder before adding. "But I love him anyway."

28

As his final semester began, Seth's life continued to return to 'normal.' His classes would take priority soon, but studying for the MCAT exam remained his focus.

The exam date had at once seemed far away, but it had rapidly approached. Weeks left to study became only days remaining. Two days prior to the exam date, Seth had been sitting in his usual spot in the library when Dave appeared. He took a seat at a study desk next to Seth.

"Can we talk for a minute?" Dave asked.

"I've got the MCAT test this weekend," Seth said. "Make it quick."

Seth didn't want to take a break. However, he was surprised by the expression on Dave's face. Dave looked worried.

"This is kind of messed up," Dave said. "But I think that you should know about it."

Seth was annoyed and moved back to his work. He didn't have time for a wild story. "So don't tell me."

"No," Dave said. "Really. You need to know."

Seth threw his hands up. His sixth sense kicked in, as if already knowing that Dave's news would not be positive.

"Every time someone has had 'messed up stuff' to tell me," Seth said. "It hasn't done me much good."

"I think that it could be okay," Dave said, catching himself. "Then again, it might not be true."

Seth scowled at Dave.

"Then why not go off and figure that out first?" Seth asked

"Because," Dave said. "It probably is true."

Seth sighed. "What is it?"

"You know that girl I've been seeing?" Dave asked.

Seth had been too distracted to understand Dave's reference. "No."

"Oh come on," Dave said. "The gorgeous babe who's been hanging on me for the past week."

Seth thought back to dinner at the cafeteria with his friends. He recalled briefly meeting someone earlier that week.

"I've seen a girl," he said. "I don't know if I would say that she was gorgeous."

Dave was not amused by the remark.

"Anyway," Dave said. "Her name's Tammy. She's friends with Rosey."

"Oh Rosey," Seth said, recalling the scene in front of Cowboys' Bar. "I saw Tony and her splitting up right before winter break."

"Did everybody see that?" Dave said. "I can't believe that I missed it."

Seth was unsympathetic.

"Love-em and leave-em Tony finally got himself left," Seth said. "He hasn't said a word about it in the couple of weeks since we've been back."

"I don't blame him," Dave said. "Anyway, I was talking with Tammy last night. She started blabbing about all this stuff Rosey had apparently said."

Seth wasn't sure where Dave could be headed. "What kind of stuff?"

"Stuff about how Tony was always lying to her," Dave said. "How he's always messing around with people's heads."

"That was breaking news?"

"It was for Rosey. Anyway, she thought that he was funny at first and played along. A month later, he wasn't funny anymore."

"And how did that relate to me?"

"Rosey said that one of the best jokes that she and Tony ever pulled off was with some flake friend of Tony's."

Seth's stomach dropped. His eyes glassed over.

Dave continued. "She said that they'd convinced this guy that his girlfriend was screwing around behind his back."

Dave waited for Seth to react, but Seth sat emotionless. "Sound like anyone you know?"

Seth felt numb. He couldn't entirely believe that Tony would play such a 'joke' on him.

"Are you kidding?" Seth asked. "Is this your own idea of a joke?"

"No," Dave said. "I don't know the whole story, but whatever you heard about April might not have been entirely true."

"Might not have been entirely true?" Seth asked, his voice turning almost sarcastic with anger. Seth rubbed his hands against his forehead.

"I'm just telling you what I heard," Dave said. "And I told you before that he's always had an eye for her."

Seth knew that he wouldn't have time to investigate the accusation, trying to figure out if what Dave was saying might be true. At the same time, he knew that if he didn't he would be distracted right up until he took the MCAT.

"Dammit," Seth said. "Couldn't you have waited to tell me?"

Dave seemed mildly offended.

"What would I be if I didn't get people the latest news?" he asked.

Seth tried to calm down. He told himself that he'd deal with things logically. He knew that Dave had only been looking out for him.

"I'm sorry," Seth said. "I just don't want to be thinking about this during the MCAT."

"I know," Dave said. "But I thought that you should know."

3:
Spring

29

Two days later, Seth reported to the MCAT testing center. He was tired, as it had been an hour long drive that morning to the nearest testing location.

Once inside the testing center, Seth was led past rows of students who were seated at individual computer workstations. The examination room was quiet, except for a soft humming sound coming from the computers.

Unlike most exams, Seth didn't have to begin the MCAT at a tightly-specific time. Because of the exam's popularity, he had needed to sign up for a time slot at the testing center several weeks in advance, so the date itself was firmly fixed. However, the amount of time that he had to complete the exam did not begin to 'count' until he had logged into the computer system.

Seth was seated amongst a mix of calm students who pecked away at their keyboards. As he entered his credentials, Seth felt agitated. He knew that he was not mentally at the top of his game. That realization had already hurt his confidence, even before beginning the exam.

Seth checked the time on wall clock and then turned his attention back to his computer screen. As he began the test, questions appeared on the screen. Seth struggled to answer them as quickly as possible.

The minutes ticked by and several hours soon passed. Seth raced to complete the remaining questions, but the test suddenly froze. A large box appeared on the screen that read: 'Time Expired - Test Complete.'

Seth slammed his fists onto his desktop. He struck with such force that his keyboard bounced with a short hop. Students on either side of Seth looked at him like he might be crazy. Seth knew that the test had gone poorly. He shrugged in embarrassment over his reaction.

30

The day after he took the MCAT, Seth was finally able to relax for the first time in what had seemed like an eternity. It was a Saturday, so his respite would only last until he decided to get to his weekend homework. Before addressing that, he'd planned to do some detective work.

Seth had only seen Tony in passing during the couple of days since Dave had told him the rumor about his being duped. He realized that it might have been for the best, since he'd wanted to speak in detail with the purported source of the rumor first.

Knowing that Rosey lived next door to April, Seth was nervous when walking up to her room. He didn't want to run into April, as the circumstances of his being near her room would be awkward.

Luckily for Seth, he needn't have worried. His trip to Rosey's door was uneventful. He knocked on her dorm room door and heard commotion inside. A moment later, the door swung open to reveal an unkempt Rosey.

"Hi Seth," Rosey said. "What can I do for you?"

Rosey looked surprised, but not unhappy to see Seth. Seth couldn't tell if her demeanor was flirty or nervous. Or both.

"I wanted to talk to you about something.

"Sure," Rosey said. "Come on in."

Seth entered Rosey's room. She took a seat on her bed and then motioned for him to join her.

"Feel free to sit down," she said.

Seth was confused and looked around the room for other places to sit. He was apprehensive about what he feared Rosey might have in mind.

"Come on silly," Rosey continued. "You think I'm going to molest you?"

"Well..." Seth said.

Rosey gave Seth a dirty look and he caved in, sitting down next to her.

"I suppose that I could guess what you're here to talk about," Rosey said. "But I'll let you tell me first."

"I wanted to talk about Tony," Seth said.

Rosey turned away from Seth, acting amused by his remark. She nervously played with several trinkets on her night stand.

"That Tony's a crazy one isn't he?" Rosey asked.

"He can be a funny guy," Seth said.

Rosey's demeanor changed. Her playful routine stopped. Seth assumed that she was resolved to coming clean.

"Here's the deal," Rosey said. "In a way he thought he was doing you a favor. In another way, you were in the middle of a mess."

"How's that?" Seth asked.

"So, April Jordan has lived next to me during our entire senior year."

Seth was confused by her stating the obvious. "Yeah, I know."

"I just want you to know what was true about what I told you," Rosey said. "April dated Bobby Jackson and broke up with him a few weeks before you started dating her."

"I knew that."

Rosey nodded. "That story I told you. The one about those two getting all freaky next door?"

Seth could hardly forget it.

"Oh," he said. "I remember."

"That really happened," Rosey said.

Seth was surprised. That was a portion of the tale that he had assumed might be nullified. His follow-up question was delivered with a weak voice. "It did?"

"It did," Rosey said. "Only not when I told you."

"When was it then?" Seth asked.

Rosey paused, as though she were trying to remember the exact timing. "It was soon after they'd broken up. Probably a week before the big dance last fall."

Seth was disappointed by the revelation, given that the timing was right around when he had first met April. He tried to lessen the blow by making a sarcastic retort.

"It wasn't a clean break up?" he said.

"Not in the least," Rosey said.

Seth looked around Rosey's room, lost in thought. He decided to steer the conversation in a new direction.

"Here's the thing," Seth said. "I'm not here to find out every detail of everything that April's done that would make me jealous or upset."

"And don't think there isn't more," Rosey said, sounding more annoyed than gossipy. "That girl has issues. She might do a good job hiding them, but they're still there."

"I need to know if I can trust her," Seth said. "That's what drove me away."

Rosey stood up and paced around the room.

"The short answer is probably," Rosey said. "The longer answer is one that I can't give you. I just don't know her that well."

"What's that supposed to mean?" Seth said.

"It means that I don't know her well enough to offer much of an opinion."

"You've lived next door to her all year and you don't know her enough to have an opinion?"

Rosey smirked.

"I've got a lot of other friends," she said. "Besides, I just gave you an opinion."

Seth was growing frustrated and tried to catch himself.

"Come on," he said.

"You two were together for a few weeks and how well do you really know her?" Rosey asked.

Seth took her question into account.

"Fine," he said. "You win."

The discussion came to an awkward pause. Seth was already starting to think about the repercussions.

"I can't say for sure what her deal was," Rosey said. "I don't think that she did anything with Bobby while you were dating."

"Did you ever see him around?" Seth asked, remembering back to the night of his breakup with April, when he had spotted

Bobby in the dorm.

"Not really," Rosey said. "One night I heard those two yelling like they might kill each other. Then she kicked him out."

"So he was still stopping by?"

"If he did, it wasn't for long. She made sure of that."

Seth thought about the other key question on his mind. As much as he wanted to know if he could trust April again, he also needed to know if he should no longer trust Tony.

"So why'd Tony have you lie to me?" Seth asked.

"Because Tony's a jerk," Rosey said.

"He must've had a reason."

"All he said was that he was looking out for you. He wanted to protect you."

Tony had never seemed the 'protective' type to Seth.

"Protect me from what?" Seth asked.

Rosey considered how to approach his question.

"You're a nice guy Seth," she said. "I'll give you the inside track on April. She doesn't have many friends because most girls on this campus think she's a little witch."

Seth knew that April didn't have many friends, but he'd never considered that other girls on campus might actively dislike her.

"Why?" he asked.

Rosey reached for an open soda can on her dresser. She motioned at her refrigerator as if to offer Seth something. He declined.

"Maybe she treated you differently," Rosey said. "I hope so."

"I'm not sure what you mean," Seth said.

"There's an air about April, like she thinks that she's above everyone else. It makes people hate her."

Seth paused, trying to take in the remark. That perception of April wasn't one that he'd felt himself, but it bothered him that April might have people trying to spite her. He stood up to leave.

"Thanks for being honest with me," Seth said. "I needed to get this cleared up."

"I really don't care anymore," Rosey said. "Tony cheated on me. So as far as I know, everything he ever said could've been a lie."

"It might have been," Seth said.

Rosey twisted her face at Seth.

"Thanks." She said, pausing. "So why is it that a nice guy like you hasn't found a new girl?"

Rosey smiled at Seth in a flirtatious way.

"Guys like me aren't very good at moving on," Seth said.

31

Seth didn't wait long to find Tony. After leaving Rosey's room, he guessed that Tony might be at the campus athletic center. Tony had played on the college baseball team in the past, somehow managing to remain academically eligible. Seth assumed that he might be practicing for the upcoming season.

The guess turned out to be correct. Seth found Tony behind a long net that hung along one side of the athletic center's indoor oval track. He was taking batting practice from one of two t-stands that he had set up. One was already empty, but the other was ready to be hit off.

Tony smiled at Seth as he approached. "One sec buddy."

After rocketing a ball off the stand, Tony put his bat down.

"You finally taking me up on that offer for some batting practice?" Tony asked

"Actually," Seth said. "I just had an interesting conversation with your ex-girlfriend."

Tony placed a fresh ball on both stands and then hit each off. He seemed only mildly interested.

"Which one?" Tony asked.

"Rosey," Seth said, not in the mood for joking around. Unfortunately, it might not have been a joke.

"What'd she have to say?"

"She said that you lied to me,"

Tony had a smug look on his face. "Oh really?"

Seth decided to get straight to the point.

"She admitted that what she'd told me about April wasn't true," he said.

"And you believed her?

Seth's voice turned cold.

"Yes," he said.

Tony continued to act disinterested. "Why would you believe anything she had to say?"

"Why would she lie to me?"

"For a million different reasons man."

Tony hit a fresh ball especially hard. Seth knew that he was getting angry.

"Name one," Seth said.

Tony let the end of his bat drop to the ground.

"She caught me with someone else," he said. "She has every reason to try to smear me."

"Why go to the trouble?" Seth asked. He knew that what Tony was saying might be possible, but it seemed the less likely truth.

Tony was surprised by Seth's aggressive tone.

"Now she's trying to turn you against me?" Tony said. "You're my friend, so she's trying to use that to get to me."

"She sounded like she wanted to forget you," Seth said. "And she wanted to apologize."

"That's a cover," Tony said. "She's trying to destroy me. Like I'm some real bad guy."

Seth picked several baseballs off of the ground and put them on Tony's tee. While he was doing that, he picked up a bat of his own. Seth didn't think that Tony would do anything crazy, but somehow felt safer holding his own bat.

Seth sarcastically asked. "And you're no bad guy?"

"You're my friend Seth," Tony said. "Why would I do something like that to you?"

Seth waited to answer. That had been the key question on his mind for days. Tony, still trying to act like their conversation was 'normal' cracked a ball off of his t-stand, sending it into the net.

"I've been thinking about that," Seth said. "I'd hoped that we were friends, but now I'm not sure what's going on."

Tony put another ball on the stand and swung at it. He didn't hit it square off of the stand, so it ended up dribbling along the ground. Seth could tell that Tony was losing his concentration.

"Forget it man," Tony said. "Forget that psycho."

"She didn't sound very psycho to me," Seth said.

"Well she is," Tony said. "I should know. I chased her around for way too long."

"I'd just like a straight answer," Seth said. "You've trashed Rosey, but you still have not given me one."

Tony motioned as though he was about to strike a bucket of balls with his bat. He then relented and regained his composure.

"So you believe her and not me?" Tony asked.

"I didn't say that," Seth said.

"You didn't have to."

"I just wanted to know some things."

"Like what?"

Seth took a deep breath.

"Like why?" he said. "Why you would you want to ruin something so good in my life by bringing it up and having her twist it?"

"I egged you on," Tony said. "I encouraged you to go after her."

"Not really," Seth said. "I remember you had a funny way of encouraging by discouraging me. Your opinion of April hasn't made much sense to me all along."

Tony stared at Seth like a cornered animal, his eyes finally wild with rage. "I never thought you'd do it. I figured you'd turn away or get shot down."

Tony looked down, as though he were ashamed. He then made eye contact with Seth and continued. "Fine. Here's the deal. It wasn't good Seth and it wasn't going to be. That girl was too much for you.

Seth's stomach sank. A small part of him had held hope that Tony might have been innocent. Instead, he seemed to be coming clean.

"What does that have to do with anything?" Seth asked.

"She just strutted around," Tony said. "Getting whatever she wanted. Making guys like me look like idiots."

Seth couldn't entirely figure out where Tony was going with his explanation.

"It wasn't right," Tony continued. "The way she treated people."

"So you wanted to punish her?" Seth asked, still trying to understand Tony's line of reasoning. "I might be confused here, but you're sounding petty."

Tony dropped his bat to the ground and let it roll to one side. It knocked into a nearby bucket of baseballs.

"I was sick of her act," Tony said. "I guess that you got in the way."

"Maybe you could have just taken a hint," Seth said. "Instead of screwing with our friendship too."

Tony looked at Seth with what seemed to be genuinely sad eyes.

"I'm sorry Seth," he said. "I just didn't handle it right. I know friends aren't supposed to be like that, but you sort of got in the way."

"You decided to trash years of friendship because you were jealous?" Seth asked. "Or mad at her? That's it?"

"I don't know man," Tony said. "It made more sense at the time. I'd hoped that you wouldn't find out. That maybe we could just forget about it."

Seth sat his bat down. He turned around to walk away, but then stopped.

"Are you completely insane?" Seth asked. "I always thought that friends weren't supposed to let a girl come between them?"

Tony didn't reply at first. He shook his head and looked down at a mess of baseballs surrounding his feet.

"I'm sorry," Tony said.

32

Seth allowed several more days to pass as he wrestled with what he should do next. It seemed logical to him to give April an explanation of what had occurred. Understandably, he was nervous regarding how that might be received, given that he was not even sure what her dating 'status' might be. Thankfully, he'd only sporadically seen her around campus, never with a guy. But an uncertainty still lingered.

Even if she was dating someone new, Seth had begun to feel resolved to apologize to her.

That debate continued in Seth's head mid-week while waiting in a line at the student union. It wasn't long until he arrived at a table full of black, plastic-wrapped packages. A worker handed Seth one of the packages and he took it to a quiet hallway.

Seth unwrapped the package and unfurled its contents to reveal a graduation gown. Graduation was still not for over two months, but the college planned for such things well in advance.

The voice of a female professor surprised Seth, coming up from behind him.

"Getting that just in case you need it Seth?" she asked.

Seth tried to be funny in response, but his reply was awkward. "You never know."

Both Seth and the professor laughed. As the professor walked away though, Seth's demeanor changed. He looked down at the gown and felt a sharp jab of sadness.

The gown was a stark reminder that his time at the college was about to end. Time would march on, regardless of any loose ends that he might have still wanted to resolve.

Seth folded the gown back up and went to the student post office. He entered a combination into his tiny post office box and found a single letter waiting inside.

Seth retrieved the letter and noticed the college's logo on the envelope. He wasn't sure what was inside, so he ripped it open immediately.

The document looked like it should have contained his MCAT test scores, but the paperwork was oddly incomplete. Affixed to the document was a note from Professor Lee, requesting a meeting.

"Oh no," Seth said.

33

Seth, along with Mark, had signed up for a fly-fishing course to fulfill a physical education requirement that Park College had in place for students. The college's scenic surroundings offered a number of unusual options. Seth had first considered taking scuba diving certification with Dave, but then opted for the more relaxing fly-fishing with Mark.

During most spring semesters, the course was front-loaded with classroom work. The thought of sitting through several sessions of 'fishing theory' had bored Seth, but he knew that they would get outside after the weather warmed up.

Luckily, the winter had turned out to be extremely mild. So much so, despite it still being early in March, the course instructor had decided to try fishing. Since then, the class had been meeting on the banks of the main river that wound through Winneshiek.

The results hadn't been successful. That said, Seth wasn't complaining about being outside for class. Mark and Seth fished next to one another along the shore, chatting between casts.

"How can you be so broken up over this?" Mark said. "You don't even know your test score."

"Lee wouldn't call me into his office for a pat on the back," Seth said. "That's not his style."

Mark cast his line and then began reeling it.

"So what," Mark said. "Forget about it. You're out here with me, right now, and you should be having a good time."

"I'm sorry," Seth said, sarcastically. "I didn't mean to ruin your day."

"What can you do about it right now anyway?"

Seth looked at Mark, not liking the advice, even if it was sensible. His meeting with Lee was scheduled for early that afternoon, so it had dominated his thoughts

"Sometimes I think that 'Just forget about it' is your solution to everything," Seth said. "Unfortunately, that hasn't exactly been working out for me."

"You aren't trying hard enough," Mark said.

Seth fiddled around with his fly lure. He'd been so distracted while talking to Mark that he had not even cast his line yet that morning. From further down the shore, Seth noticed the instructor giving him a curious gaze.

"You decide what you're going to do about April yet?" Mark asked.

"That's on my mind too," Seth said. "You see Tony around?"

Mark shook his head. "He's been under the radar over the past couple of days. Dave's not too happy with him and, when I see him, we're going to have an interesting chat."

"He said that he was sorry," Seth said, a hint of sarcasm in his voice.

"You know," Mark said, changing the subject. "The only time this year that I ever saw you happy was when you were with April."

"What're you talking about?" Seth asked.

"I mean," Mark said. "That was the only time when you weren't whining about how bad your life was or stressed out over every test."

Although Seth had briefed Mark on recent events, he had not suggested much in the way of a course of action. The obvious question had revolved around trying to patch things up with April.

"Now you're saying that the key to happiness is running back to her?" Seth asked.

"I've changed my mind," Mark said. "You gave me new information on the situation."

"You don't know everything about her," Seth said.

"I know enough," Mark said. "It sounds like she's not as bad for you as I'd originally thought."

Seth suspected that Mark knew about some of his other, earlier issues with April. At the very least, Melissa would have likely shared some elements of their post-winter break conversation.

"I just don't know," Seth said.

"You know that you were wrong about the main reason that you broke up with her," Mark said. "It seems to me that now you're scared to try to patch things up."

"Maybe, but I think that it's too late now. I screwed things up with her."

"It's never too late Seth."

"What if she's moved on?"

Mark smiled. "She hasn't moved on,"

"How do you know?" Seth asked.

Mark winked at Seth. "I had Dave check it out."

Seth felt oddly relieved by the confirmation, but the feeling didn't last for long. He still wasn't sure if April would accept any explanations or apologies from him.

Mark helped Seth finally get his lure into place. Seth cast out. Mark followed a moment later.

"Why did you like her so much Seth?" Mark asked.

Seth remembered back to the first few times that he had interacted with April. He had been stressed and uncomfortable with the attention, but it had also been a uniquely positive experience for him.

"At first it was exciting," he said.

"Oh yeah," Mark said, a grin forming on his face. "Hottest girl on campus."

Seth gave Mark a cynical look.

"After Melissa," Mark said. "Of course."

"As I got to know her more, she impressed me. In a lot of ways, she was a better person than I am. At least she probably has a bigger heart. Maybe I thought that I'd learn something."

"I thought that you did learn some things?"

"Yeah. Maybe a little too late."

Seth reeled in his line, but he was not paying it much attention.

"Was it worth it?" Mark asked

Seth didn't understand the question. "Was what worth it?"

"All the hassle," Mark said. "Looking back, do you regret having dated her?"

Seth's answer came out so quickly that he surprised

himself. "No. I don't regret it."

Mark reeled in his line and cast it out again. Seth sat down on a rock, thinking through what he needed to do next.

34

Despite still being concerned about his meeting with Lee, Seth left his fishing class feeling energized about his situation with April. He began to plan a trip to her room for later that day, but he did not end up having to wait that long.

Seth noticed April seated on a bench that was installed near the campus library. He could see that she was taking down a note in her planner. Seth, feeling confident, crossed the lawn to where she was seated.

After arriving, Seth stood over her and said. "Hi."

April slowly looked up at Seth. Her eyes didn't seem to register any emotion toward him, either positive or negative.

"Hello," April said. Her voice was cold.

"I just thought I'd come over and say 'Hi,'" Seth said.

"Well," April said. "You've done that."

"Uh-huh."

The two were silent for a long moment in what seemed to Seth to be a battle of wills. Seth ultimately broke the tension.

"Look," Seth said. "You shouldn't just cut people off."

April seemed surprised by the statement. Much to Seth's dismay, she grew angry.

"Excuse me?" April asked. "You accused me of cheating on you and flipped out."

April put her head down, returning to writing in her planner.

"That's not fair," Seth said.

"What was not fair?" April asked. "The part where you didn't even give me a chance to respond? The part where you went crazy on me?"

"This might sound pathetic, but I need to tell you that I was off base about everything that I said."

"You're right," April said. "That does sound pathetic. You think admitting that you were wrong three months later can patch things up between us?"

Seth could sense that he was quickly losing control of the situation. He'd underestimated how angry April was with him.

"No," he said.

April let out a short, sarcastic laugh.

"I think that you do," she said. "Well, it doesn't work that easily Seth. What you said hurt me more than you'll ever know."

"Why didn't you tell me that it wasn't true?"

"I tried to. You weren't listening to me, remember? You seemed to have somehow made up your mind in advance. Would it have really mattered if I'd continued to deny it?"

Seth sat down on the bench next to April. She slid over from him.

"It might've helped," Seth said.

"No," April said. "You freaked me out. You'd already accepted what you wanted to believe."

"I wanted to know the truth."

"The truth was that you'd become a weirdo. What kind of guy goes around, trying to dig up stuff from my past?"

The charge made Seth angry. So far as he was concerned, he'd not tried to find out if April was cheating on him. The accusation had landed in his lap.

"That's not what happened," Seth said.

"How was it then?" April asked.

Seth was speechless. He was being scolded. Amid April's barrage of anger, he struggled to get his thoughts in order.

"I was told some things that weren't true, Seth said. "I was also confused about some things that you'd said had happened."

"We've all done things in the past that we regret," April said. "But to say those kinds of things about me…"

April's voice trailed off. Seth thought that she might cry and put his hand on her shoulder. She quickly brushed it away.

"I know," Seth said. "I know that I screwed up."

"Do you?" April asked.

"More now than ever before. I'm sorry."

April slid her planner into a pocket of her backpack.

"That's great Seth," April said. "Maybe the next time you meet a girl, you'll remember that."

April stood up and walked away. Seth, still shell-shocked from the encounter, let her go without another word.

35

At the appointed time of his meeting, Seth took a seat in a chair adjacent to Professor Lee's desk. Lee turned around to face him, papers in hand.

"You can always take a year off," Lee said. "I'm sure that you'd get in if you retook the MCAT and reapplied."

"So you think there isn't any chance for next fall?" Seth asked.

"You might still get on a waiting list," Lee said. "Otherwise, you can reapply next year. Those are probably your options right now."

Seth let the news hit him. He had just been told that his scores on the MCAT had been too low for the top medical schools.

"That's not something that I've planned for," Seth said, feeling panicked at the idea of deferring for a year. It might have been common practice, but he had no idea what he would do during that 'gap' year.

"You could easily get into one of the tier-two schools," Lee said. "But I wouldn't recommend it. You have too much potential."

"I've worked too hard to settle for that," Seth said.

Lee gave Seth a fatherly look.

"Yes," he said. "You have."

"You don't think that I should bother submitting my applications?" Seth asked.

"You should still apply. You still might get in. However, I think that your applications will be longshots. You need to plan for that being the case."

Seth shook his head in disappointment.

"And then we wait?" Seth asked.

"We'll know more in a few weeks," Lee said.

Professor Lee sat the test-related papers aside. He stared at Seth. "Have you spoken with anyone yet about what's going on in your personal life?"

Seth gave Lee a confused look. "What do you mean?"

"We have discussed this several times during the past few months," Lee said. "You've slid after three extraordinary years."

"There were some things going on," Seth said. "But it's all became a lot clearer recently."

Professor Lee looked relieved.

"I hope so," he said. "For your sake. You can't afford any further distractions."

"Do you think I can still make it?" Seth said.

"Yes. Eventually. If you don't give up."

Seth looked out the window at the grove of trees near where he and April had been briefly sitting earlier in the afternoon. Seth turned back in Lee's direction and found the professor still focused on him.

"I've made a lot of mistakes," Seth said.

"Second chances happen," Lee said. "But you need patience."

"What if I screw up again?" Seth asked.

"Then you keep trying until you get things right," Lee said. "Don't give up on what you want the most."

Seth stood up to leave the office. He glanced again at the grove of trees.

"Thank you sir," Seth said. "You've helped clear up some things that I've had on my mind today."

"That's what I'm here for Seth," Lee said.

Professor Lee turned around to continue working as Seth exited the room.

36

Seth knocked on April's door and waited. He was terrified, knowing that what he had in mind could backfire. His heart pounded so hard in his chest that he worried for a moment that he might pass out.

Given how his earlier conversation with April had gone, Seth had assumed that the odds would be against him. Nevertheless, he knew that he needed to try.

April swung her room door open to find Seth standing in the hallway. At first, she looked surprised, but that initial reaction quickly changed to anger.

"Why are you here?" April asked.

"I wanted to talk about why I've been an idiot," Seth said.

"We did that already. We don't need to go over it again."

April began shutting her door, but Seth put his palm against it to stop her.

"Look," Seth said, pleading. "Just give me a minute."

"I don't want to waste the time for either of us," April said.

Seth was desperate to say what he needed to say. "Please."

After another moment's thought, April relented.

"Fine," she said.

Seth stepped into April's room. It had not changed much in the several months since Seth's last visit, but he still felt out of place there. He took a seat in a chair and tried to compose in his head what he wanted to say.

April remained standing. She didn't give Seth much time to think.

"What is this?" April asked "What's so important?"

Seth looked into April's eyes. Over the past several days, he'd gone over several different 'plans' in his mind. He'd hoped to be tactful, but most of what he had rehearsed felt scripted. He knew that he'd only have one chance.

Despite the urge to rehearse a speech endlessly, Seth had feared that his words would lose their meaning that way. In the end, he decided to be bold and honest.

Seth quietly told April. "I'm in love with you."

April looked away from Seth, offering no reaction at first. His heart continued to race as he waited for her response. When she finally did speak, she didn't look at him.

"You don't know what you're talking about," April said. "Good grief."

Her voice sounded odd to Seth. He couldn't tell if April's voice was quivering, like she was about to cry, or if she was mocking him.

"I know exactly what I'm telling you," Seth said.

Seth held his gaze on April, waiting for her to look back at him. When she did, she looked composed. Seth wondered if she hadn't been taken by his words.

"How can you say that?" April asked. "It sounds ridiculous."

"It doesn't to me," Seth said.

"What does that mean?"

Seth took his time. He had an answer for her, but he wanted to get it right.

"I've had a long time to think this over," Seth said. "I realized why I've cared for you since we first met."

April continued to seem skeptical.

"Seth," she said. "Love doesn't work that way."

"Why not?" Seth asked. "How do you know? How does anyone know?"

"It just doesn't," April said. "Love takes time."

Seth again stared into April's eyes. This time he spoke with confidence.

"My whole world was different with you," Seth said. "You were unlike anybody I'd ever known."

April's demeanor finally began to soften.

"You pushed me to think in ways that I never would've without you and I want to build on that," Seth continued. "I was a better person with you than I ever could be alone. You made me that person."

April rubbed tears away from her eyes. When she spoke, she said her words with humility. "You can't put people on pedestals Seth."

"But I'm not putting you on a pedestal," Seth said. "I'm telling you that I respect and care for you. I'm not looking for someone who's perfect. I'm looking for someone like you."

"That's not true. That's not what you told me before."

April moved to sit on her bed. Seth walked over and sat next to her. She pushed him away as he tried to console her.

"I made a mistake," Seth said. "A lot of mistakes. I won't make them again. Sometimes people get confused. Sometimes they have to figure things out."

"What happens next month when one of your friends comes up with something that makes you jealous?"

Seth held April close.

"That won't happen," he said.

April still didn't seem convinced.

"I can't put my heart into this just to have it broken again," April said.

"I don't want that either," Seth said.

When April looked into Seth's eyes, she appeared uncharacteristically vulnerable to him.

"I don't want to have you and lose you again," she said.

"You won't," Seth said.

"How do I know that?"

"You have to reach out and take a chance. I didn't trust you or believe in you enough. I've learned from my mistakes and my fears. Now I'm asking you for the chance to use what I've learned."

April pulled Seth tightly to her in an embrace. They shared a passionate kiss that was filled with pent up emotion.

37

Seth and April quickly fell into familiar routines, resuming the wonderful aspects of the times that they had previously experienced together. As had been the case in the past, they both worked to juggle their time together with their other obligations.

Often, they found themselves strolling to a park nearby campus, taking advantage of the crisp spring weather. Seth and April would ride next to each other on a large swing set at the park. Each rising up into the air, higher and higher, competing like little kids.

Seth was still busy studying or finalizing his medical school applications, but they managed to find the time to spend together.

Unlike when he'd previously dated April, Seth made a better effort at including his friends in the relationship. For example, it became common for Seth and April to have lunch with Mark and Melissa. Even Dave had seemed to strike up an unusually friendly rapport with April.

Seth had a nostalgic side to him that crept out as he entered the final weeks of the semester. He knew that he would miss his friends and his daily routines at Park College. It didn't help his facing that transition after his post-graduation plans had become so muddied. Time marched on, a fact illustrated best one day during an early dinner at the cafeteria.

Mark took a seat at a table already occupied by Dave, Seth, and Melissa. He held up an envelope.

"Moment of truth," he said.

"What's that?" Dave asked.

"You know that job that I applied for at the school district over in Winnebago?" Mark said.

Seth had witnessed Mark applying for numerous teaching positions, all to no avail. It had been disappointing for everyone. Unfortunately, Seth had never wanted to be 'right' about his warnings to Mark to take his studies more seriously.

With the school year ending and most students having found jobs, it had been hard for Seth to see Mark scramble. Not all of Mark's friends had realized the efforts that he had undertaken. Dave, for instance, looked confused by Mark's question.

"Sure," Dave said.

"This is their reply," Mark said.

"Hurry up and open it," Melissa said.

Mark opened the letter and read it to himself. He showed no emotion and then sat the letter down.

Melissa glanced at the piece of paper. Everyone assumed that it had been another rejection letter.

"I'm sorry," Melissa said. "You'll get the next one."

"Yeah," Mark said. "Winnebago's football team had better watch out this year."

"Why's that?" Dave asked.

"Because Washington's got a new history teacher to coach the best program in the conference," Mark said.

Mark reached into his coat and pulled out a different letter. "It came earlier this morning."

Melissa hugged Mark.

"I'm so proud of you babe," she said.

"Congratulations," Mark said.

Dave sat his glass down hard enough to grab everyone's attention.

"You're always stealing my thunder," Dave said. "Aren't you?"

Seth wasn't sure if Dave was truly upset or if his dramatic question had been an act. It didn't seem like anyone else at the table knew either.

Mark laughed uncomfortably. "What do you mean?"

A wide smile crossed Dave's face.

"I just found out that I have a fellowship for a Ph.D program at Princeton," Dave said.

Everyone at the table was surprised, but congratulatory.

"Wow," Seth said. "To study what?"

"Drugs," Dave said.

"You're getting a Ph.D in drugs?" Seth said.

"Not weed man," Dave said. "the prescription stuff."

Seth smiled and backed off. Dave had talked about becoming a pharmacist in the past. After all, he'd had several science classes with Seth. Still, Seth was disappointed in himself for not being more aware of Dave's shifting plans. Amid everything else happening in Seth's life, he was struck by how he had lost track of his friends' basic life plans.

"Seth," Mark said. "You hear anything yet?"

"I'm still waiting to hear from Mayo," Seth said. "Iowa, and Pacific."

Mark had a concerned look on his face. "Kind of getting down to the wire isn't it?"

"Yeah," Seth said. "But you know how it is."

"I'm sure it'll work out Seth," Melissa said.

Seth replied, "I hope so."

Silence swept over the table as the individuals reverted attention back to their meals.

Things didn't remain mundane for long. Dave suddenly jerked his head up from looking at his tray. Everyone turned and waited for him to speak.

"Guys!" Dave said. "I've finally figured out how to make that chick stock market work!"

38

A few days later, Seth and April had plans for a low-key Friday evening together. Seth arrived early at the Philadelphia Bar and Grill. He read a newspaper while waiting for her. A bartender didn't take long to ask Seth for his order.

"Can I get you anything?" the bartender asked.

"Just some cheese curds for now," Seth said. "I'm waiting for my girlfriend before ordering food."

It still felt weird to Seth when he referred to April as his 'girlfriend.'

"Sound's great," the bartender said. "Just give me a shout when you're ready."

After the bartender left, Seth returned to his newspaper. He only paid passing attention when the restaurant's front door swung wide open. Tony stumbled inside. He looked like he'd been sweating profusely.

Tony staggered over to where Seth was seated and collapsed into the booth's empty seat. Seth looked up from his paper in annoyance.

"I'm so glad you're here," Tony said, slurring his words. "I need to talk to you buddy."

"I'm not your buddy Tony," Seth said. "I don't want to talk."

"No," Tony said. "You don't understand. I really messed up this time. I need someone who I can trust."

Seth, along with Mark and Dave, had largely kept their distance from Tony. Because of their nearing graduation and everything associated with the significant life changes that would soon take place, keeping a distance had not been difficult.

With April arriving at any moment, Seth wanted Tony to leave.

"We had trust once," Seth said. "You threw that away."

"Come off it," he said. "You can't sit there and ignore me."

"I'm sorry," Seth said. "But I don't care about whatever problem you might have."

Tony, although disoriented, seemed genuinely hurt by the remark.

"Some friend you turned out to be," Tony said.

"No Tony," Seth said. "You made your choices. Now you're going to have to live with them."

Tony stood up, looking stunned. He tried to reach over and put his hand on Seth's shoulder, but Seth brushed it aside.

"Just leave," Seth said.

Tony staggered past Seth's table and headed toward the front door.

As Tony exited the restaurant, April passed through the doorway, sliding around him. Tony glanced up and down at her.

"You'll never know what you missed," Tony said.

April slammed the restaurant door shut on Tony.

"You won't either," April said. "Dirt bag."

39

Mark slipped on a tuxedo coat and straightened his tie. Seth helped him with the back of his collar.

They were in their room, preparing for the spring ball.

"How many formal balls does this college have in a school year?" Mark said. "Didn't we just have one?"

"That was last November," Seth said.

Mark sighed. "Sign of the times then. Man, this year's been flying by."

Seth helped Mark tighten his tie.

"That it has," Seth said.

With Mark ready, Seth unzipped a rental bag from Aumannson's Clothing and produced the same white tuxedo that he had worn to the autumn ball. Mark noticed it and gave Seth a confused look.

"They run out again?" Mark asked.

It took Seth a second to realize what Mark had meant. He gave a shrug in reply.

"It's for good luck," Seth said.

"Uh-huh," Mark said.

While getting dressed, Seth grabbed his phone and called April. As soon as she answered, he asked. "Are you ready to go?"

"No," April said, sounding distracted. "Don't rush. I just finished showering. I'll need another thirty minutes."

"Okay," Seth said. "See you soon. Love you."

Seth hung up the phone.

Mark looked stunned. "Whoa! When did this happen?"

"What?" Seth asked.

"We're already at 'Love you?'" Mark said. "When did that

happen?"

"Things progress and I guess that I forgot to tell you." Seth smiled. "I'll fill you and Melissa in later."

Seth put on his tux jacket.

"Leaving already?" Mark asked

"April's not ready yet," Seth said. "But I might as well head over. It's a nice night out."

Mark nodded. "I'll see you at the ball."

Seth was walking on the sidewalk in front of April's dorm when he glanced up at April's window. The curtains were shut, but the lights in her room were on, creating a silhouette effect against the drapes.

A shape that looked like April stepped in front of the window. A moment later, another shape stepped into view, but it looked like a large male joining her.

Seth had been blissfully thinking about the wonderful evening that he intended to have with April, but the sight at her window made his smile disappear. As Seth watched, the two silhouettes moved together.

The male seemed to be holding April. She moved up toward him, appearing to kiss him. A moment later, April-like shape disappeared out of view. The male figure followed.

Seth was shocked senseless. He couldn't believe that April would cheat on him, not after everything that they had recently been through. Yet, he could not deny what he had just witnessed.

Seth's demeanor quickly changed from shock and sadness to anger. He was furious for being played like a fool and he walked quickly toward April's dorm room.

When Seth arrived outside April's room, he knocked at the door. There was no answer, but Seth could hear movement inside. The sounds made Seth's blood boil.

Seth shouted through the door. "April! It's me!"

After another second, Seth heard more commotion inside. Briefly, he heard April's voice.

"Seth!" she said. "He's hurting me!"

April's voice sounded muffled and then went silent.

The cry made Seth realize that he'd misunderstood what was occurring in April's room. He immediately tried twisting the doorknob open, but it was locked. Seth tried pounding on the door and even tried to kick it open, but the metal frame would not budge.

Seth yelled. "Open the door right now!"

Seth continued kicking as hard at the door. He caused a loud commotion in the hallway, but no one peered out from the nearby rooms to help him. Given the timing, many students would have already left for the ball. Others might have chosen to ignore the noise out of fear.

Seth kept pounding on the door. He was about to kick it again when it opened wide. In a split second, Seth saw Bobby holding the door and April lying on her bed, her clothes torn.

In a flash, Seth surmised the situation. In that same instance, Bobby grabbed Seth by the arm and threw him onto the room's floor. Bobby then slammed April's room door shut.

Seth scrambled onto his feet. Before he could do anything else, Bobby's fist hurtled toward his face.

Seth ducked to avoid the blow and rushed at Bobby with all of his might, hoping to knock Bobby down. The effort was only modestly successful as Seth's momentum caused him to lose his balance. Both men fell to the floor.

Bobby was stronger than Seth and stood up first. Seth, still shocked from the unexpected events of the past several seconds, staggered to his feet. He could smell alcohol on Bobby.

Seth realized that, if Bobby was drunk, he could use that to his advantage. Bobby took another wide swing at Seth, but he was slow and Seth was able to avoid the brunt of the blow. Nevertheless, Bobby's punch still grazed Seth's shoulder and stung. Even if Bobby was drunk, Seth could tell that he was hitting hard.

Seth became creative and stepped near April's closet. It had a door in front where Seth subtly laid his hand. When Bobby leaned in for another punch, Seth grabbed the door's handle and opened it onto Bobby's face.

The pain from that strike seemed to enrage Bobby. He pushed Seth back like he was made out of straw. Seth tumbled onto his back in the middle of the room's floor. Towering from above, Bobby stared down at Seth like a wild animal. Bobby moved in for the kill.

Seemingly out of nowhere, the flat, thin edge of a racquetball racquet swung straight into the center of Bobby's face. The sharp attack threw him off balance. Seth used the opening to kick upward at Bobby, landing a solid attack.

Dazed, Bobby fell hard onto his back, right into the middle of April's closet. On his way down, Bobby's head hit the concrete rear wall of the closet. The impact knocked him unconscious, with his body collapsing atop a pile of clothes.

Seth rushed over to April, who still had a tight grip on the racquet. He held her in his arms as she cried. Overcome by pain and emotion, Seth also began to cry.

"Are you okay?" Seth asked.

"I think so," April said. "I'm lucky that you made it here when you did."

"What happened?" Seth asked.

"There was a knock at the door," April said. "I thought that it was you, but it turned out to be Bobby. He pushed his way inside."

"Did he hurt you?" Seth asked, referring to April's tattered clothes. The side of her face looked swollen.

"I'll be okay," April said. "That personal self-defense class paid off, at least long enough to yell for help. He sure looked surprised when you arrived."

In the middle of the embrace, the room door opened. Campus security rushed inside.

"What's going on here?" the lead security officer said. "There have been calls of a disturbance."

One of the junior officers pointed the lead security officer in the direction of Bobby's unconscious body. He was still unmoving in the closet, covered with clothes.

"Someone has some explaining to do," the lead security officer said.

Through their tears, Seth and April both tried to smile.

40

Within minutes, Bobby was starting to come around and was helped to his feet. He was led out of April's room in handcuffs by two police officers.

April sat with an ice pack on the side of her face. Her cheek was swollen, but it didn't look bad. The lead security officer was about to leave.

"Thanks for cooperating with us," the lead security officer said. "The police are waiting for you down at the station. It could be a long night."

"No problem," Seth said.

The officers all turned to leave. When April and Seth didn't move, the lead security officer looked confused. He asked "Are you coming?"

April motioned to Seth.

"Yes," she said. "I'll have him drive me down in a minute."

Seth looked surprised.

"Are you sure Miss?" the lead security officer said. "We really need to get this report finished. I'm sure that you want it to be over too."

"I do," April said. "I just want a minute or two alone. Is that okay?"

"Not a problem," the lead security officer said. "We'll be waiting for you two down at the station."

The officer exited, leaving Seth alone with April. Seth hugged April close. They gave one another long, thoughtful looks.

"You sure you're okay?" Seth asked.

"I'll be fine," April said. "I'm just a little shook up."

Seth gave April a disappointed look.

"I'm sorry that we didn't make it to the ball," he said.

"It's not your fault," April said, a wry smile on her face.

Abruptly, April stood up and began riffling through her clothes.

"What're you doing?" Seth asked.

"We should go to it," April said. "You're not the only sentimental one. It's important to me."

Seth's mind was still focused on the need for them to get down to the police station. He couldn't imagine what else April might have in mind. "Where did you want to go?"

"The ball," April said, winking at Seth. "Just for one dance. Then we can go talk with the police."

Seth was surprised, but not disappointed by the suggestion. He'd been looking forward to the evening as a chance to replace some of the memories of disappointment that still lingered from the last ball. In some ways, he'd managed to do that already, at least in regards to handling Bobby.

"Are you sure?" Seth asked. "After what you've just been through?"

April pulled out the dress that she had worn to the prior ball.

"That's why it's important," April said.

41

April and Seth passed through the glass doors of the campus recreation center and strolled through its deserted lobby. They could hear the DJ announce that the last dance of the evening was about to begin.

"Perfect timing," April said.

Seth smiled.

The music started as April and Seth entered the dance area. They began moving together in a slow dance, Seth holding April close. As they turned through the crowd, Seth noticed several familiar faces.

When he felt an unexpected poke at his back, Seth turned around to see who was trying to get his attention. It was Rosey, dancing with a partner of her own.

"Good to see you back on your feet Seth," Rosey said.

"Thanks," Seth said, noting the irony of the remark as it related to the evening's earlier events. "Nice to see you too."

Rosey turned to April.

"Hi April," Rosey said.

April seemed surprised by the warm greeting, but smiled right back.

"Hi Rosey," April said.

As the music continued to play, Seth noticed Tony standing alone in the distance. He was seemingly the only person not dancing. Seth decided not to linger his attention on him and turned back to April.

Seth soon heard a voice yell out his name through the music. He looked around until he noticed Melissa waving at him while she danced with Mark.

Mark yelled to Seth. "About time you got here!"

"Better late than never," Seth said.

Dave, coming out of nowhere, interrupted.

"You get mugged on the way to the forum?" Dave asked.

"It's a long story," Seth said.

Dave smiled.

"I'd like to hear it," he said.

"You will," Seth said.

Seth looked back to April. Even after everything she'd been through that evening, she still looked as beautiful as she did the last time that Seth had danced with her. The music soon hit its climax, at which point Seth and April both leaned in to kiss.

42

Monday afternoon following the ball, Seth was seated nervously in Professor Lee's office. Lee sat across from Seth and pulled several printouts together before speaking.

"I won't dance around this," Lee said. "Pacific is the only school that has called, they've admitted you."

Seth was disappointed, but not crushed.

"It's a good school Seth," Lee said.

"It's not what I wanted," Seth said.

"I've looked into your situation further and have reconsidered my earlier advice. I'd recommend that you start there. It will be difficult, but you may be able to transfer elsewhere if things go well after a year."

Seth was surprised by the recommendation and would need time to consider it. At first, all he could say was. "Okay."

Seth had come into the meeting with other things to discuss with Lee. He hadn't been sure how to bring them up, but he felt like this might be the right opportunity.

"To be honest sir," Seth continued. "I've been having second thoughts about my motivation for pursuing medical school."

"What do you mean?" Lee asked.

"I think that I may have gone into this for the wrong reasons."

Lee appeared confused by Seth's statements.

"You've told me about your father Seth," Lee said. "I know how much you becoming a doctor meant to him. That's a very honorable motivation."

"But it's meant such a sacrifice for me," Seth said.

Lee gave Seth a hard look. Seth knew that, after going on the journey toward medical school over the past four years, Lee was bound to be disappointed with Seth's statement. As such, Seth was pleasantly surprised by Lee's next words.

"Of course," Lee said. "There are other ways to honor his memory."

"I need to do what will make me happy," Seth said. "I'm not saying that I don't love the medical profession or that I want to quit. I just want to make sure that I'm choosing the right path for the right reasons."

"As well you should," Lee said. "But I want to caution you against rash decisions."

Lee had inadvertently hit on the heart of the matter for Seth.

"That's my biggest fear right now," Seth said. "There are so many decisions to make that I don't know if I have the right answers."

"You'll know the right answers when you see them," Lee said.

Seth thought about this remark for a moment.

"Can I ask you a personal question?" Seth asked.

"By all means," Lee said.

"Is it all really worth it?"

Seth had spoken with Lee in the past about his own career focus. Lee had devoted much of his life to being an educator. In getting to his position, Lee had forgone opportunities that might have led to a more traditional family role for him.

"Only you can answer that question," Lee said. "You won't know the answer until you're there."

"How did you choose?" Seth asked.

"We devote ourselves to what we love. I love teaching and helping students."

"Even at the expense of a family?"

Lee smiled at Seth.

"That was my choice," Lee said. "I've never had a family, but I've never been lonely. Most people have to search hard to realize what they want to do with themselves in life."

"And how do I discover what that is?" Seth asked.

"You either know it now or you will when you find it," Lee said. "Just don't let life 'happen' to you Seth. Seek out your opportunities and make the most of the ones that come your way."

Seth nodded. Lee shook Seth's hand as he stood up. As he reached for the office door, Seth halted before exiting.

"Do I have to choose one opportunity over the other?" Seth asked.

"I never said that you had to," Lee said. "It's just harder if you don't. Much harder."

43

Park College ended spring final exams several days before the actual graduation ceremony. This 'gap' allowed time for professors to tabulate final grades. It also gave the graduating seniors several last days with one another.

Many parties broke out during that time, with many students partaking in those last opportunities to cut loose. Other students spent the time in quieter fashion, enjoying the company of friends who would soon no longer be daily fixtures in their lives.

Predictably, Seth fell into that latter category. He continued to spend time with his friends and, of course, April.

On the evening before graduation, Seth and April had a final dinner in Winneshiek at the cafe where they had eaten during their first date. Seth and April faced one another in the same booth where they had enjoyed a long conversation after ice skating together.

Their banter and conversation was still as comfortable as ever, but the mood was somber.

"And where do we go from here?" Seth asked.

"You're asking me?" April responded.

Seth furrowed his brow. He chuckled, hoping to lighten the mood. "You mean that you don't know either?"

"Of course not, "April said.

Seth thought about all of the advice that his friends had given him and how this moment had lingered in the back of his mind since meeting April. He knew that his relationship with her might end up being fleeting, as the winds of change blew into their lives. Ready or not, they would have hard choices to make that would determine if they stayed together after graduation.

"Someone once told me that these things always happened at the worst possible time," Seth said.

As the words came out of his mouth, Seth thought about just how large of an understatement it had been.

"Isn't that the truth," April said. "Have you told your parents or Professor Lee yet about your decision?"

"No," Seth said. "I was planning on telling them tomorrow, maybe after the ceremony."

Graduation day was bittersweet for Seth. The academic year ended with his life circumstances in a dramatically different place than he would have ever expected during the prior autumn.

Seth felt numb throughout most of the actual ceremony. He watched so many familiar faces quickly pass through the diploma line. After the formal festivities had ended, the crowd cleared out of the stands. The campus football field filled with students, professors, and families. Everyone mixed together, forming a blanket of bodies.

From across the crowd, Seth spotted Professor Lee. The two cut through the throngs of people between them and reached out to one another.

"You should be proud of everything you've accomplished Seth," Professor Lee said.

"Thank you," Seth said. "I'm proudest of the last thing I learned."

"And what was that?" Lee asked.

"I'm leaving this school knowing what it means to be happy," Seth said.

The pair shook hands and hugged. As Seth walked away, Professor Lee called out.

"Where are you going Seth?" Lee asked.

"I'm taking some time off," Seth said. "To figure out the rest."

Seth smiled and turned away from Professor Lee. He then stepped past the fringe of the crowd, where he was joined by April.

Seth reached out for April's hand. They walked together, away from the field and into the future.

Author's Remarks

Like Seth, my romantic experiences were few and far between during college. Thus, it was ironic that in writing a story with my college experiences in mind, I wrote one with such a significant romantic foundation. In truth, I spent nights at college wishing that I had a girl like April in my life. Like many stories, this one was rooted in those thoughts of what might have been.

When I first approached writing this story, I found myself considering if it should be comedic or dramatic. I wasn't overly familiar with many fictional books about the modern college experience, but I was familiar with films that covered such periods. Such films often took either the comedy path – "Animal House" and "Revenge of the Nerds" - or the romantic drama route – examples might have included elements of "Rules of Attraction" or even aspects of "Good Will Hunting."

Drama and romance ended up being the driving force of the story for me. Like many college dramas, the theme of finding one's self was part of this story.

One surprising influence that the story owed much to was Kevin Smith's low-budget comeback film "Chasing Amy." The issues raised in that film, such as mistakes made in one's life, forgiveness from others for those mistakes, and bitter conflicts between close friends were all story elements reflected in this book. I found some relation to those topics in my life and thought that I could comment on them.

The story's original title, "A Girl from Another World," was taken from the title of the second chapter of the novel "Doctor Zhivago." Although that title inadvertently conveyed to some the expectation of science fiction elements, it actually directly referenced Seth's intimidation that April was from a higher 'class' than him. That theme of class was one that pervaded "Doctor Zhivago," even if my story developed into something entirely different. A certain somber mood and the winter setting did remain from that masterpiece's influence.

Most who have been to college would agree that romantic doings end up being a large part of that life. This story tried to mirror that reality. As was the case in real life, romantic topics found their way into so many conversations in this story - albeit some at the level of gossip.

Certain readers may be surprised when I say that the outlandish events that happened in this story were likely the most rooted in real life. If you thought something to be hokey or sappy or generally not believable, the sad thing was that it probably actually happened to someone in my memories.

In most cases, events that I heard about or experienced myself were twisted or tweaked just enough to make them fit within the narrative. This was not to say that the core of the experiences weren't kept honest to what occurred. Rather, it meant that I didn't want to be sued by anyone.

The dialogue was often true to how I had discussed certain subjects with people during my college years. Of course, none of the characters were directly based on anyone whom I knew during that time. Rather, the characters were amalgamations of many different pieces from the personalities of many, many people whom I knew throughout college.

Friends might read this story and notice a personality trait that reminded them of someone, but to assume that a particular person embodied a particular character would be an error. Each character was a creation, as was the world that they inhabited.

Further, some elements of the story revolved around medical school and its application process. I admit to being rather loose in the actual timeframe that one needs to follow in this process. I did that for dramatic reasons and ask those who might have been more familiar with that process to indulge me.

As is often the case, most of what I wrote was from what I knew.

What I hope did unfold on the page were scenes of friendship, conflict, comedy, betrayal, mudslinging, a touch of violence, and, at its heart, a romance. I hope that you found this story to be a roller-coaster ride that you enjoyed.

Thank you.

Daniel Christensen
Ellendale, Minnesota